CHAPTER 1

Jules

Whenever teachers or coaches would talk to my dad about me, they would say, "That Jules sure is a leader," or "Your daughter certainly is assertive." Everyone else would say I was *bossy*. People claim to not like a bossy person, until it comes to a day like today, when they just crave someone to tell them what to do. So that's what I'm doing. I am running this tragic show because no one else wants to take the reins; everyone else is so emotionally distraught they aren't capable of anything beyond basic functions, and even being sure everyone is eating enough and staying hydrated has somehow fallen on my shoulders.

I'm not just ordering everyone around, though. I'm also the shoulder everyone seems to be crying on. I comfort my sister-in-law, Laurel, who sobs as I remind her of how much Dylan loved her. So many relatives have come up to me, seemingly trying to comfort me and yet in an instant falling apart and sobbing to me that they can't believe Dylan is gone or what a shock it has been. I keep repeating the same lines of how fortunate we all were to have the time we did with Dylan.

In the midst of final preparations for the service, I feel a tug at the hem of my black dress. Evie, my four-year-old, looks up at me, beckoning me closer. I kneel down and she whispers, "Can we play on the slide?" The church where we're having the service has a little playground outside. I am so relieved to be able to have the small reprieve, leaving our grieving, bewildered family members inside while Evie and I take a few minutes to just enjoy ourselves outside during a break in the rain.

Someone comes outside and asks me, "Jules, should we be starting now?" My back is turned, so I roll my eyes and grumble to myself, *Was my itinerary not clear enough? Can you not read a clock? Figure it out yourself.* I take a breath, look at my watch for show, then turn and say, "Yes, in about ten minutes. We'll be in in two."

Less than ten minutes later, Evie and I take our place at the front pew with the rest of the family members. I settle Evie on my lap, wanting to hold her as close to me as possible. She snuggles in, the large crowd of people making her understandably nervous.

I've been wearing a lot of hats today – funeral director, supportive sister-in-law, grief counselor, mom. As the service progresses, we approach the part when I will speak, when I will have to assume the role that I have been trying to avoid acknowledging all day – widow.

What everyone tells me is that they want me to give the eulogy because I am the person Dylan loved the most and the person who loved Dylan the most. It makes sense. I'm the mother of his child; we were together for ten years and married for five. But I know that what everyone is really thinking is that I talk the most, more than anyone should, and today that's what they want. They want to hear my long, detailed, many-faceted stories about Dylan. And I'm more than willing to comply, because if I can keep thinking about, talking about, living in the past, in the life I had with Dylan, it gives me more time to escape thinking about what comes next. More time to avoid facing a life without Dylan.

When we come to my part in the service I lift Evie from my lap, and I feel that I am losing the one weight that has been keeping me grounded. I settle Evie on my dad's lap, and I see her wrap her arms around his neck, looking as if she might fall asleep on her *Bobpa* -

Through Anything

KC WEBER

ISBN: 9798834273264

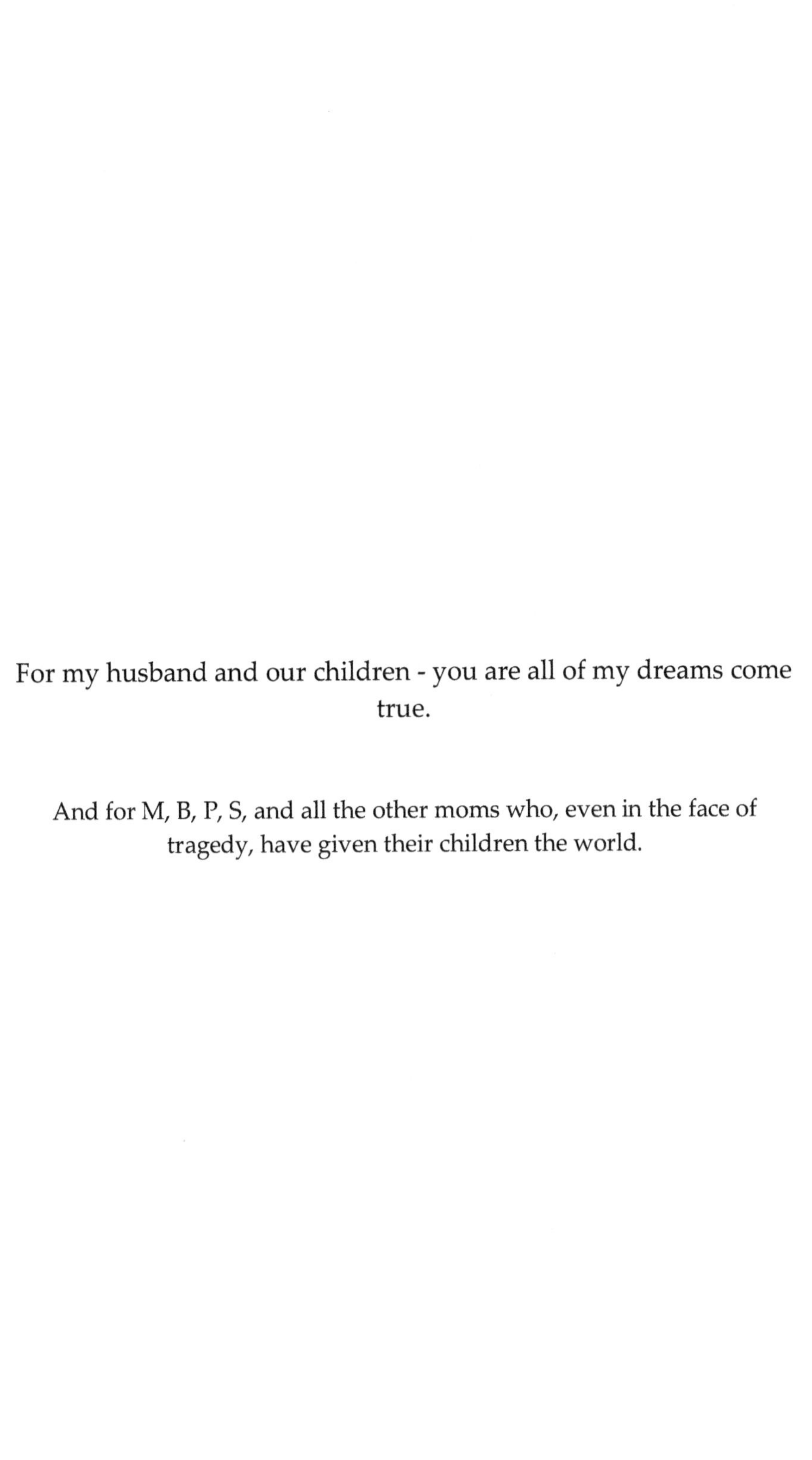

For my husband and our children - you are all of my dreams come true.

And for M, B, P, S, and all the other moms who, even in the face of tragedy, have given their children the world.

'Grandpa Robert' was far too difficult when she was learning to talk. My dad gives my hand a squeeze for courage, and I squeeze back.

In my worst nightmares I never could have imagined I would be here. That at the age of 28 I would lose Dylan, my husband, my best friend, the man I have loved for ten years, my daughter's father.

As I walk to the lectern, I feel hundreds of eyes on my back, and I can feel the crushing weight of their pity. I make every effort to show them that I do not need their pity. That I can and I will survive this. That I will not fail Dylan, no matter what.

Towards the end of the eulogy my eyes hover across the crowd, and I spot a lone figure standing at the back of the room. My eye catches his, and the pain I recognize in his dark eyes - pain that reflects my own - nearly overwhelms me. I stumble over my words for the first time. I quickly check my notes, find my place and recover. When I look up again he is gone.

I stand in Evie's doorway, watching her sleep, finally feeling a moment of calm after a very trying day. I hear a series of heavy knocks on the door. I sigh, already guessing who it is. I had a feeling he would be stopping by tonight.

"Hey, Jake," I say opening the door and automatically stepping out of the way. Jake stumbles through the door. He is a wreck, just like I had expected him to be. Everything on him, from his short blond curls to his dress shoes, is sopping wet; it's January in Eugene and he's not even wearing a jacket. The half-empty fifth of what looks like whiskey swinging from his hand seems to explain part of his disheveled appearance. Losing his best friend five days ago explains the rest.

"Keep your voice down. Evie's asleep," I remind him quietly, taking his elbow and leading him to the kitchen table.

"Asleep? I wanted to see her... see my goddaughter," he slurs, plopping down in a chair.

"It's 10PM, Jake, she's been asleep for hours. And I wouldn't want her seeing you like... this," I say gesturing at his inebriated self. "You can see her in the morning."

He scowls at me and raises the bottle as if he means to take another drink. I snatch the bottle from his hand, unscrew the cap and take a sip. Then I tip the bottle back and take a gulp. Jake raises his eyebrows at me. I hardly ever drink. And I definitely don't drink whiskey or whatever this is. I put the bottle on the counter, out of Jake's reach, and ignore the burning in my throat.

"Where've you been?" I ask. "I didn't see you after the service."

"I walked around town. Saw some of our old spots," he says vaguely.

Stopped at all of Dylan's and your old favorite bars, you mean, I chuckle to myself.

"Thought I'd come here. See if I could crash just like the old days."

He's come to crash at our house like he did every University of Oregon home football game weekend for the past however many years. At least I don't have to worry about convincing him that trying to find his way back to his hotel isn't a good idea.

"You can crash here," I say. "But you have to stay on the couch. Evie took your room years ago," I say teasingly, though he doesn't seem to catch the joke.

He nods. "I know. Thanks, Jules."

I lead him toward the couch wrapping his arm around my shoulders so I can bear some of his weight. Jake is tall, broad, and muscular, so I'm struggling a bit under his weight; we're moving slowly but making progress.

"Look at this. I'm already breaking my promise to Dylan," I hear him mutter.

"What do you mean?"

"He made me promise I'd take care of you. And already you're the one taking care of me."

~~~

Jake

"There he is," Dylan called across the hospital room; I stood in the doorway unsure of my next move. Jules stood from the chair next to
~~~

Dylan's bed and motioned for me to take her place.

"I'm going to grab a coffee down in the cafeteria," Jules said, placing a soft kiss on Dylan's forehead. "You have my number if you need me, Jake." She patted my arm reassuringly as she passed me.

"How's she doing?" I asked once Jules had left the room, which I knew she had done purposefully to give Dylan and me some privacy.

Dylan sighed. "Tough as nails. Taking on every burden in the world like it's her personal responsibility. You know."

"So, the usual," I said with a small grin. Dylan nodded with a smile that didn't reach his eyes.

His face fell as he continued to stare at the door Jules had just walked through.

"Please take care of her. Of them. My girls. Please take care of them," Dylan said, eyes still trained on the door.

My voice cracked as I answered. "You know I will. I would do anything for your girls, Dylan."

His lips curled up in a small smile. "I know you would, Jake."

~~~

Jules

I shake my head. Dylan couldn't have been serious when he asked Jake to take care of me. *Jake could never take care of me,* I scoff to myself. *Just look at him. He can't even take care of himself.*

I get Jake settled on the couch and lay a blanket on him. As I turn to walk away he grabs my hand. Eyes still closed, he asks, "How am I going to get through this?"

I bend down and say quietly, "You can get through anything, Jake. I know you can. You've been through worse." He gives a semi-nod and by the time I cross the room I can hear him snoring.

I walk down the hall to my bedroom. Like I've done the past few nights, I wrap myself in Dylan's robe before I crawl into my too-big, too-cold, too-quiet bed.

Hearing Jake's snores from the other room makes me laugh with dark humor. *I'm a widow. Why am I still being kept awake by a man snoring?*
~~~

CHAPTER 2

Jake

"What are you doing?" I hear Jules ask from the door of the kitchen. She's wearing sweatpants and an over-sized, faded University of Oregon sweatshirt that must be Dylan's, her curly blond hair up in a knot at the top of her head.

"Cooking. What does it look like I'm doing?"

"You don't cook. I lived with you for a year and I never once saw you cook something." She's right. Dylan, Jules, and I lived together when they were both getting their master's degrees in education and I was finishing my fifth-year architecture program. Dylan and Jules have been living in the house we rented ever since. In the year I lived here I never cooked. Not once. I was surprised this morning to learn the house has a gas stove.

"That was years ago. I've learned a lot in the years since you were my *roomie*." Jules rolls her eyes. She always hated when I called her that, which just made me do it even more. I grin at her irritation. "And one thing I've learned is how to cook a damn good omelet. Does Evie like omelets?" I ask.

"I don't think she's ever tried one. She'll be up any minute." Jules glances down the hall then says more quietly, "Just a heads up that she's been pretty quiet lately. She's barely said a word the past few days, so don't take it personally if she doesn't say much."

I nod, turning back to the stove, my chest feeling tight with emotion knowing that my sweet girl is hurting. Jules walks away, making me think Evie must have woken up. I hear two sets of feet walking down the hall; I paint a smile on my face that I hope looks real enough. Evie steps into the kitchen.

"There's sleeping beauty. Morning, Evelyn," I say brightly to my goddaughter, trying not to choke up at the sight of her. With her dark hair and blue eyes, she is the spitting image of Dylan, even down to her freckles. Her curls, which happen to be an adorable frizzy mess this morning, are the only trait she shares with Jules.

"Uncle Jake!" she squeals hurtling toward me. I snatch her up into a hug. "Did you make me breakfast?" she asks. Jules looks shocked that Evie is talking to me.

"I sure did. Plop yourself in a chair, missy, and I'll serve it up."

"What'd you make, Uncle Jake? What'd you make?" she asks hopping up and down in her chair.

"Your breakfast, your highness," I say dramatically, bowing as I place a plate in front of her. "A delicious ham and cheese omelet." Evie's eyes light up as I hand her a tiny, kid-size fork. Jules gapes at Evie as she devours her omelet.

"I guess the kid likes omelets," I whisper to Jules.

"And her Uncle Jake," Jules says with a small smile, never taking her eyes off of Evie. I feel pretty proud that I managed to get Evie talking and eating breakfast this morning.

"What are we doing today, Uncle Jake?" Evie asks me around a mouthful of omelet.

I look at Jules. "I'm not sure what your mom has planned, sweet pea."

"We're going to the park, like I promised," Jules tells Evie.

"You come too, Uncle Jake!" Evie says excitedly. "You can push me on the swing."

I look out the window, confused. "But isn't it raining?"

Jules rolls her eyes at me. "If we waited until it stopped raining to go to the park we would be waiting until July." She's exaggerating, but I guess she has a point. Kids growing up in Eugene must just be used to playing in the rain. "Besides, what's the point of having sparkly pink rainboots and a unicorn raincoat if you never get to really use them?" Jules asks Evie, tickling her.

"I think I left my raincoat at my hotel," I say, rubbing the back of my neck sheepishly. *Or is it at the first bar I stopped at?* "I'll go grab it and meet you at the park."

At the front door, Jules whispers at me, "Be sure to change, too. You smell like you dove head first into a whiskey-filled swimming pool."

I whisper back at her, "It was bourbon."

I arrive at the park, freshly showered, in clean and dry clothes, wearing the raincoat I thankfully found in my hotel room. As I approach the little playground, I notice Evie stomping around in a puddle in her sparkly pink rainboots. I hand Jules the coffee I picked up for her on my way over to the park. She nods her thanks at me, eyes never leaving Evie.

"Look at me, Uncle Jake!" Evie calls to me.

"Wow! Look at you, sweet pea!" I call back. "What am I supposed to notice?" I whisper to Jules.

"Who knows. She just wants you to watch her. It doesn't matter what she's doing. She could just be sitting quietly and she would still say 'Look at me.' She would love it if I would just stare at her falling asleep. Just being a kid," Jules says chuckling.

"Well it's nice to see her having fun, hear her talking."

Jules nods. "Thank you for that," she says quietly. Neither of us speaks for a minute as we sip our coffees and watch Evie play, enjoying her own make-believe world. Jules is uncharacteristically quiet, and I wonder if Evie isn't the only one not speaking a lot these days.

"I'm sorry about last night, Jules," I begin hesitantly.

"I have a lot of experience dealing with your drunk ass. At least this time you had an excuse," she says flatly.

I shake my head. She's right. She has dealt with drunk me a lot – in college, when I lived with Dylan and her, and even on the frequent occasions I would visit Dylan in Eugene after I moved away.

"So what are your plans now that..." I can't finish the sentence.

"I'm taking this week off of work, then heading back next week."

"So soon?" I ask surprised.

Jules shrugs. "It will help getting back into a routine. Evie will go back to preschool next week, too. She needs it. I need it."

"I guess that makes sense," I say, remembering how much a routine, staying busy, can help. "How's the whole work and preschool routine going to work with ... um... just you?" I ask awkwardly.

"Not sure, but I won't have to figure out how to do the whole single caregiver routine on my own quite yet. I won't be going it alone for a while; my dad is going to stay with us for the next month."

Thank God he wasn't at Jules's house last night. Robert Nelson defines intimidating. I'm sure if he had gotten one look of my *drunk ass*, as Jules so aptly put it, he would have slammed the door in my face. I might have spent the night on the front lawn.

"What are you going to do after that?" I ask.

"Dylan's mom mentioned something about maybe coming over from Redmond to help out, but we'll see if that pans out." She doesn't sound too optimistic. "Once my dad leaves I guess I'll just have to figure out how to survive as a single parent on my own."

"Do you need me to help out for a few weeks after your dad leaves?"

"What?" she asks, looking at me for the first time since I arrived.

"I could take a few weeks off of work. The owners of JT Architects are pretty chill," I say, smiling at my own joke. My dad and I are pretty chill. "I could stay somewhere close by and help with things like getting Evie to and from school. And I could even put my newly acquired cooking skills to work. I may know how to cook a few things beyond omelets." *Or at least I could* learn *to cook a few things beyond omelets.* Jules gapes at me, seemingly stunned by my offer. "What?"

"I'm just... I'm just surprised to hear that from you. I guess I thought we wouldn't see much of you anymore now that Dylan…" She trails off and looks away.

"Hey," I say stepping in front of her so she has to look at me. "We were friends first, remember?"

~~~

"Hey, Jake." Dylan, my randomly assigned roommate stood in our doorway. Even though we had only met a few days before we were becoming fast friends. "I heard from a guy down the hall there's some A cappella concert happening on the quad tonight. Do you want to go?"

I shrugged. "Sure, why not."

Dylan and I approached the quad, which was surprisingly packed with people.

"Do you think we can find a spot?" Dylan asked looking a little disappointed.

I scanned the crowd and my eyes landed on long, curly blond hair that I would have recognized anywhere. "I found us a spot," I said, grinning, leading Dylan through the crowd. I plopped down on the blanket next to Jules. She turned to me startled by the body that suddenly appeared on her blanket. Then realizing it was me she smiled at me, and I wrapped her in a tight hug.

"Hi, Jake. I was wondering when I would run into you."

I had known Jules since middle school. From back when she had braces and wore blue eye shadow. We both grew up in Bend, Oregon. We ran in the same circle of friends in middle and high school and now we were both in school at University of Oregon. We had only been on campus a few days, but it was still great to see a familiar face.

"Aren't you going to introduce me to your friend?" I asked grinning at the pretty brunette sitting next to Jules.

Jules gave me a hard look. "This is my roommate, Megan," Jules said through gritted teeth. "Megan, this is Jake, an old friend." Jules looked past me to Dylan. She stuck her hand out toward him for a handshake. "Hi, I'm Jules." Dylan seemed to still be recovering from his shock at seeing me sit down on what he thought was just some random girl's blanket.
~~~

"Dylan, nice to meet you. I'm Jake's roommate."

I noticed Dylan and Jules grasped hands a little longer than is normally socially acceptable. And when I looked at Jules her cheeks had gone a little pink. That's interesting, I thought, my eyebrows raised in surprise.

"Jules!" someone yelled from across the way. Jules looked up, saw who had called her, and waved excitedly.

"I'll be right back. Callie's over there," Jules said smiling and getting up from the blanket. Callie, Jules's older sister was a junior at U of O.

"Oh, Callie's over there. Maybe I should go say hi, too," I said, giving Jules a mischievous grin. I had been teasing Jules about how hot her older sister was for years, and I wasn't stopping now.

"You stay where you are. I'll be right back," Jules said, annoyed. She leaned down and hissed at me, "Behave yourself while I'm gone, Jacob."

"What's that supposed to mean?" I hissed back. I knew what she meant, but she inclined her head toward Megan to be sure her message was perfectly clear.

While Jules was gone, I scooted myself closer to Megan and started chatting her up, more because Jules told me not to than out of actual interest. When Jules came back she gave me a scathing look, but she didn't say anything. I was surprised she didn't make me scoot back to my spot by Dylan. Instead she sat down between Dylan and me. Jules leaned over and hissed in my ear, "Seriously, Jake, stop. I have to live with this girl for a year. Don't ruin it for me the first week. Hands off."

I narrowed my eyes at her. Her dark brown eyes met my gaze, not backing down. Jules knew me too well, and she was definitely right to not want me to get involved with her roommate. As I told all the girls I got involved with, I was absolutely not interested in anything serious with anyone. And I probably never would be.

"Fine," I muttered.

Throughout the concert I noticed Jules and Dylan chatting quite a bit. Or at least Jules was talking non-stop as always and Dylan seemed completely enthralled. At one point I saw their phones come out and it looked like they had exchanged numbers. Very interesting, I thought to myself, frowning. So I can't mess around with her roommate but she can take an interest in mine? The same rules don't apply to Jules? But then I thought more about it and came to the conclusion that with my reputation, that rule really should only apply to me.

When we were back in our dorm, Dylan asked me, "Hey, Jake, I was just wondering if there's anything going on between you and your friend Jules."

"Me and Jules? No. Nothing," I said.

"You two just seem really close, so I wasn't sure."

"I've known her forever," I explained. "She's just a really good friend. A really bossy friend," I added chuckling.

"OK, I just wanted to check because..." Dylan hesitated, "because she gave me her number." So I was right they had exchanged numbers, but still Jules giving Dylan her number surprised me. Really surprised me. Jules had never dated anyone in high school, not from lack of trying on several guys' part.

"And I just wanted to be sure it was cool with you before I called her. Bros before hos, right?" Dylan said with a small smile.

"What did you just call her?" I roared at him.

Dylan looked horrified. "I didn't mean...It's just an expression...I just meant that friends come first... and I mean..." he sputtered.

I slapped his shoulder, grinning. "I'm just messing with you. I knew what you meant." I was impressed that Dylan had checked with me before pursuing anything with Jules. It seemed to be an indication of the kind of friend he was, the kind of guy he was. "Dude, there's nothing going on between Jules and me," I said honestly. "She's beautiful; no denying that." Dylan knew I wasn't blind, so I couldn't deny that she was gorgeous. "Good luck, man. If you're interested in Miss Bossy then good luck," I said, laughing. Then more seriously, I said, "Really, Dylan, she's a great girl. The best." Dylan nodded at me hesitantly. I leaned closer and growled at him, "And if you hurt her I'll cut your dick off."

~~~

Jules

I can't hide my surprise that Jake is offering to help me in the coming months. I honestly was surprised he was still at our house this morning, certain that he would already be on his way home. I
~~~

was even more surprised when he arrived at the park like he said he would; I lost a silent bet with myself, predicting that Jake would message with some excuse explaining he wouldn't be able to join us after all. Even though I'm still surprised, I realize I'm glad he's here. Even hungover, embarrassed Jake as company is preferable to standing at this park completely alone.

Of course, Jake and I have spent a lot of time together over the past several years, but only because our relationships with Dylan have brought us together. There was a time, a long time ago, when Jake and I were close friends, just on our own. But that was years ago. His offer to help me out, to even take time off of work for me, is so unexpected and truthfully quite touching.

But I know it's not really me he's here for. It's Evie. His goddaughter. He's worried about his goddaughter and wants to do his part to support her. It's sweet to think that he is taking the role of godfather so seriously, that he cares so much about her.

Jake's not the only one worried about Evie. I'm terrified. What will her life be like now that she only has one parent and the parent she's left with is *me*? In my darkest moments I think Evie would have been much better off if the roles had been reversed and Dylan were the one still here for her.

Dylan was the most incredible father; without him I am highly aware of all of my shortcomings as a parent. While I lose interest in playing with kid toys within a few minutes, Dylan could spend hours building with Duplos or creating elaborate worlds of imagination mixing action figures with princesses and ponies. He could turn even the most mundane activity, like a grocery shopping trip into an exciting adventure, while with me a grocery shopping trip is just a grocery shopping trip. In the times when I was at my wits end with Evie's preschooler attitude Dylan always swooped in with his patient demeanor, calming both Evie and me. And I'll never be able to bark "Evelyn Grace!" in quite the same commanding tone as Dylan could.

How am I going to do this without him? Evie deserves so much more than just … me. But we'll have to figure it out somehow, because from now on it really is just the two of us.

Jake

"That's a really thoughtful offer, Jake," Jules says. "I'll… I'll see how things go the next few months."

It's not a yes, but I'll take it. I smile at her and she offers me a small smile in return.

After a few quiet moments, Jules admits, "I just can't imagine doing this on my own forever. Once the school year's over Evie and I are moving in with my dad."

"He's going to love that," I say smiling softly. Jules and her sister Callie have always had their dad wrapped around their fingers. I'm sure he is head over heels for his granddaughter, too.

"I know," Jules says smiling softly. "He offered before I even had to ask. It will be nice to have Dylan's family only a half hour away in Redmond, too."

I had a feeling Jules would be moving back to our hometown of Bend so that she would have some more family support from her sister and dad. "What about work?" I ask.

"I'm going to finish out the school year here. Once the school year's over I'll resign from my position. I called Sarah yesterday." Sarah was a year ahead of us in high school and went through the same teaching program Jules did. She now works at an elementary school in Bend. "I asked her if she knew of any teaching positions that might open up in the area. It turns out someone's retiring from her school so they have a position for me next year if I want it. It's not ideal because it's kindergarten, and five-year-olds are practically feral."

I scoff. "Feral? Newsflash, Jules. You're living with an almost five-year-old," I say pointing at her daughter running around the playground who will turn five in October.

"I know! And it's hard enough dealing with just one of her. Imagine 30 of her. In one small room. All. Day. Long."

I shudder, dramatically. "What a nightmare," I say theatrically. "Not your ideal grade level, but it gets you into the school. That's amazing, Jules," I say elbowing her good-naturedly. Leave it to Jules to have everything mapped out less than a week after losing her husband. I'm impressed, but I can't say that I'm surprised. "It will be good to have you home."

"That was always the plan. For us to move back to central Oregon," she says with the slightest tremor in her voice. I know she means it was Dylan's and her plan. "*This* obviously wasn't the plan," Jules sighs. "But at least I can follow through with something he wanted."

Jules and Evie moving to Bend makes it possible for me to follow through on something Dylan wanted, too. I may be doing a crap job of it so far, but I intend to keep my promise to Dylan. I *will* take care of Jules and Evie.

CHAPTER 3

Jake

I'm sitting on the Nelsons' front porch waiting, a cooler full of chilled sodas beside me. I haven't been here in years, probably since high school, but it looks exactly how I remember it. Though I doubt there are still boyband posters hanging in Jules's room.

Callie and her husband Ryan are milling around the front yard waiting for Jules, Evie, and Mr. Nelson, to arrive. Jules has been so cryptic about whether or not she needs help with her move. Even though I offered to help her move multiple times, it's like she's allergic to asking for help. I was so frustrated with Jules's resistance to my help with this cross-state move, I finally called her sister Callie and asked what time I should show up to help everyone unload the moving van, acting as though Jules had already invited me. It's not the first time I've had to be less than honest to find a way to help Jules out.

~~~

During the spring I offered so many times to come help out with Evie, but Jules always said she didn't need help, that she was managing. So I
~~~

had to try some deceptive tactics. I sent her a message, crossing my fingers that my idea would work.

> *JAKE: Hey, Jules, I'm heading to Eugene this weekend to catch the Ducks' basketball game. While I'm there is there anything I can do to help?*
> *JULES: Yes! Evie would love for you to take her to preschool one day*
> *JAKE: Great! And I'll make dinner one night*
> *JULES: OK that would be wonderful. Thank you*

I ended up buying tickets to several U of O basketball games and other games for random sports I didn't even care about just so that I could have a reason to go over to Eugene. For some reason Jules was fine with me helping out – dropping Evie at preschool, taking her to the park so Jules could have a break, cooking dinner – as long as helping out wasn't the main reason I was in town. Every time I visited, Jules was thrilled to have the help, but she couldn't admit she needed or even wanted it.

~~~

I see Jules's car turn the corner and am surprised to see Robert is driving it. Around the corner comes the 15-foot rental truck with Jules at the helm. Even at 5'8" she looks so tiny at the wheel. I'm impressed that she made the three-hour trip from Eugene in that beast, but I stopped being surprised by what Jules can do a long time ago.

Once she parks at the curb I walk over to the truck and stick my head through the open window. Jules looks even tinier up close in the giant cab of the truck wearing an oversized U of O t-shirt that must be Dylan's. "What are you doing here?" she asks smiling.

"I thought you might need some extra muscle," I say flexing. Jules shakes her head at my lame joke.

"I'm glad you're here," she admits. "Loading up with just my dad and me was a lot harder than I expected. It will be nice to have some more help on this end."

I want to say, *I offered to drive over to Eugene and help but you*
~~~

wouldn't let me, but I bite my tongue. She looks exhausted and doesn't need me scolding her. Jules unbuckles and hops down from the cab, stretching her arms above her head and yawning.

"You look like you need a nap or some caffeine."

"A nap will have to wait, but some caffeine would help," Jules sighs.

"I have sodas in that cooler if you want me to grab you something," I offer, pointing to the cooler I left on the front porch. "I made sure to have lots of Dr. Pepper."

Jules's eyes light up. "My favorite! I'd love one."

I know it's your favorite, that's the only reason why I bought it, nasty cough syrupy stuff, I think to myself. "I'll grab you one."

"Thanks, Jake. And thanks for coming. I have to get Evie out of the car and settled in the house then I'll come back out and we can get started."

"Good. We need you to tell us what to do. Your favorite thing," I say elbowing her.

After a few minutes getting Evie settled in the house, Jules opens the back door of the moving truck and we set to work.

"Does this go upstairs?" I ask Jules, nodding my head at the box I'm carrying that reads *Jules Bedroom.*

She rolls her eyes. "That has been a topic of heated debate for the past few months. My dad insists that I take the downstairs master. I insist that I don't. We ended up settling it with a coin toss. And I lost."

"So downstairs bedroom?" I ask.

"Yup," she mutters, clearly not pleased to have lost that argument.

The rest of the afternoon goes smoothly. Jules directs our small crew on what goes where. *So gifted at bossing everyone around,* I chuckle to myself. Ryan and I move most of the heavy furniture, and I am baffled by how Jules and Mr. Nelson managed to load everything on their own back in Eugene. Callie and Mr. Nelson take turns watching Evie, unloading when they aren't on kid-duty. Jules unloads and directs, stopping for only a few seconds at a time to take sips of her Dr. Pepper.

At one point I step out of the rental truck holding Jules's guitar case. "Hey! This looks familiar," I exclaim, raising the case as Jules and I pass each other on my way into the house. When I lived with Dylan and Jules, she would play her guitar and sing most evenings. Dylan would sing along with her or just watch her, mesmerized. Occasionally, if I was in a very good mood, they would convince me to strum along on my guitar. Looking back I realize how special those nights were, and that I should have joined in more often.

She offers a smile that doesn't reach her eyes. "Right. That's probably horribly out of tune."

"Does the altitude change do something to guitar strings?" I ask, trying to understand her meaning.

"I just haven't played it for… a while," she says cryptically. *Oh. Maybe without her biggest fan around anymore, she hasn't felt much like playing.*

Once the truck is unloaded Jules has to return it to the rental company's local location.

"I'll follow you and give you a ride back," I suggest.

"I don't want to take up any more of your time, Jake," Jules says checking her watch. "I'm sure you have other things to do," she adds with a guilty look on her face.

"Jules, this is exactly what I planned to do today – help out a lifelong friend. There is nowhere else I'd rather be. Will you please just let me help you," I huff.

She looks taken aback. "OK, thanks, Jake. That ride would really help." She turns back to her family. "Hey guys what kind of pizza do you want me to pick up?" she calls at them.

There's a chorus of different answers. "Meat lovers." "Veggie." "Pepperoni." She pulls out her phone to make the order.

"How about you?" Jules asks me as she types in the number.

"Me?"

"Yeah you," she says looking up from her phone. "What kind of pizza do you want?" she asks with a small smile.

"Oh, um…anything's fine," I say, surprised and unexpectedly pleased to be included in the family dinner plans.

Jules is pretty quiet in the car as I drive back to her house. Usually a complete chatterbox, Jules has been a lot quieter these past few months. Which I supposed is to be expected after devastating loss.

"I'm sorry to take up your whole Saturday, Jake," Jules says finally, breaking the silence.

"Stop saying that. It's not like I had anything else planned," I reply.

"Evie and I won't make it too long past dinner," she says yawning again. "So you can probably still have a real Saturday night."

"A real Saturday night? What's that?" I ask confused by her comment.

"I don't know. Whatever eternal bachelors like you get up to on the weekends," she says shrugging.

"*Eternal* bachelors?" I echo, laughing. "I think the word you are looking for is *handsome. Handsome* bachelors." Jules rolls her eyes at me, which just makes me laugh even more. "And what do you think we *handsome, eternal* bachelors get up to on a Saturday night?" *This should be good,* I think, curious what she imagines I do on the weekends.

"Probably a lot of sports and bars, sports bars just so you can kill two birds with one stone," she says without having to even think about it.

Well shit, that's so spot-on it's like she's been spying on me.

"And maybe spending some time with the flavor of the month, if you feel like it," she adds.

Well that part's not entirely accurate. Or at least maybe it was somewhat true a few years ago, but not so much recently.

"Well I'll give you the sports, bars, and sports bars," I say with a grin. "That's pretty accurate."

"Oh, so not owning up to the flavor-of-the-month description, then," she says, one eyebrow raised. "The university opening must have been exciting for you. A whole new school of young, pretty fishies to hunt."

I open my mouth to respond, but Jules suddenly says, "Don't miss the turn!"

I fly past the intersection where she wants me to turn. "Nope, Miss New-In-Town," I say with a superior smile. "That's their *old* location. They moved to a new spot years ago."

Jules frowns and slumps back in her seat; I know she hates being wrong about *anything.* I realize a little too late that with what an exhausting and emotional day this has been I probably should tone down the teasing. And I know whatever she's thinking about, worrying about, it isn't the new location of the pizza place.

Jules

Moving back here was definitely the right decision. I loved living in Eugene, but I have really missed central Oregon. And I have so much support raising Evie here; between my dad and Callie I know she will always be in good hands. Evie and I barely limped through the past few months just the two of us. My sister always seemed to know when I needed her and made a few surprise weekend visits that really helped us through. The few U of O home games that brought Jake into town helped, too; even if omelets wouldn't be my first choice for dinner, he was a big help whenever he happened to be in Eugene.

Still I can't escape the feeling that this isn't right. I always have the thought in the back of my mind that Dylan should be here. That he should be having these experiences, too - moving into a new house, getting reacquainted with the city and discovering all of its changes.

For at least three years, Dylan and I had been talking about and planning when we would move back to central Oregon. But there weren't too many teaching positions open, and we both were lucky to have great jobs in Eugene.

Then when more teaching positions opened up, Dylan insisted he wanted to stay in Eugene just two more years to see a special class of students from the high school basketball team he coached through their senior year. As fate would have it, Dylan was too sick to even attend one game of that class's senior season. It was gut-wrenching, but I managed to make it through the team's special tribute to Coach Bailey at their end of season gathering.

Now I find myself having all of these experiences, big and small – big like packing up the house we lived in when we brought Evie home from the hospital into a rental truck and moving across the state, small like discovering that my go-to pizza delivery place has moved locations –without Dylan. And my overwhelming thought is that I wish I weren't doing this alone.

Jake

"What's up?" I ask Jules after a few quiet moments, unable to take her silence.

Jules rakes her fingers through her hair, a habit that becomes more frequent when she's anxious or overwhelmed. "It's just hard starting over," she sighs. "Even if this is my home town, I'm still starting over. Different city, different job, different school for Evie. Making new friends or trying to resurrect old friendships. It's just a lot."

I mull over her words a bit. "I know exactly what you mean. I had to start over when I moved back here, too." She looks at me, eyes wide with surprise. I shrug. "I had to navigate what it was like to move back here after college. The city had changed, friends had moved away and weren't coming back. It's this weird limbo of things being the same but not the same." And even though there is nowhere else I'd rather be –my family is here, our family business is here, I love this place - there have been a lot of times when I've felt overwhelmingly lonely. Jules moving back into town actually widens my social circle considerably.

"But don't worry," I say patting her knee. "You'll figure it all out in no time, and you have me as your tour guide until you do."

She nods, giving me a thoughtful look. "That's right. I'm glad I have you, Jake."

Back at the Nelsons' house, Jules is putting together Evie's dinner plate while Callie sets out plates and napkins. I start getting drinks for everyone.

"Can I get you something to drink, Mr. Nelson?" I ask.

"Oh my God, Jake, you're not 15, call him Robert," Jules calls over her shoulder. I look back at her dad and from the look he is giving me I can tell he would prefer it if we were not on a first name basis. He has always intimidated me with his gruff voice and the way he's always scowling at me. Even now that I'm taller, bigger, stronger than he is, I feel myself shrinking under his steely glare.

"Jules is right, Jacob, call me Robert," he says slowly. "And I'll have a seltzer water."

I nod and duck my head into the fridge, glad to be momentarily guarded from Robert's glare. *What did I do?* I ask myself. But remembering that he's known me since I was a teenager, there are number of things I've done that he could easily take issue with.

As we gather around the table, Callie raises her glass, and we all raise our glasses following suit. Even Evie raises her little plastic cup. "To our newest Bend residents," Callie begins. "We're so glad to have you home," she says, her voice warbling with the tears she is holding back.

Jules offers Callie a reassuring smile. It is impossible not to feel the love between these two sisters, how they are communicating through an unspoken language in a way only the closest of siblings can. My throat feels thick thinking about how precious that innate connection is, and I am grateful when my train of thought is interrupted by Evie violently knocking her cup into my glass making Jules laugh and the table call, "Cheers."

CHAPTER 4

Jake

It's only Wednesday and I am already looking forward to the weekend. I've been swamped with work all summer. A lot of construction happens in the summer months, and I have several building sites to check on a daily basis to answer questions or verify that JT Architects' designs are being interpreted and followed correctly - basically that no one is screwing up my plans. I haven't had a full weekend off in the past two months, but this weekend my schedule is slowing down enough I will actually be able to take both days off.

I haven't seen too much of Jules and Evie since their move in late June. I've been able to meet up with them to play with Evie at a park between job site visits a few times, but that's about it. On my drive home I realize that the coming weekend is one of the last weekends in August. I've barely seen Evie or Jules this whole summer, and they're starting school in just a few weeks. I know I need to fix that; I haven't been the friend I told Jules I would be. She probably chalks my absence up to sports, bars, sports bars, and some notion about a non-existent "flavor of the month."

On my drive I spot a car with something attached to its roof rack that gives me an idea. I call Jules right away, unable to wait until I get home to put my plan into action.

"Hey stranger," Jules answers, in a voice that I hope is pleasantly surprised. I wince at the term *stranger*, but I know with how little she's seen me this summer it's deserved.

"Hey, Jules! I was just looking at the calendar and I realized your summer vacation is coming to an end soon."

"Ugh don't remind me," Jules groans. *Teachers. Months off and they complain for weeks that their vacation is* almost *over,* I laugh to myself. My mom, a 30-plus year teacher has been complaining since August 1st about having to go back to work in September.

"Sorry," I say, not at all sorry. "Anyway, with your summer winding down, I was wondering if you and Evie have any plans this weekend."

"We've been hitting up a different park most mornings, trying to get outside as much as possible but beat the heat. I was just planning to do more of the same this weekend. Other than that, no plans."

"You have plans now. Saturday 8AM. I'm picking you girls up. And I won't take no for an answer."

"Is that right?" Jules says, and I can almost hear her roll her eyes, annoyed that I'm the one telling her what to do. "And what are these *plans*?"

"Just know that we'll be going to a park. A special park. It's not too far away. Bring sunscreen and wear a swimsuit." Jules doesn't say anything, and I know she's hesitating. "Just roll with it, Jules, OK? Sometimes surprises can be fun. And for once you could just let someone else call the shots."

I hear her sigh, and I grin because I know she's going to cave. "OK. Saturday 8AM. We'll be ready. Swimsuits and all."

I punch the air in silent victory.

"Do you need me to pack a lunch for everyone?" she asks, thoughtful as ever.

"Nope. I've got it covered." I remember something important that I almost overlooked. "One more question: How much does Evie weigh?"

It's silent. "Yeah that sounded totally weird," I say, grimacing, but I hear Jules chuckling. "I just want to make sure I get the right size lifejacket for Evie."

"Now *that* sounds more reasonable," Jules says with a laugh. She gives me the information, and I change course heading to the sporting goods store. "Whatever you have planned, I'm sure Evie will be thrilled. And I'm looking forward to it, too, Jake. Thanks for thinking of us."

Her simple thanks make me regret even more that I haven't spent enough time with them this summer. I hope she hasn't felt like I've forgotten about her while I've been so busy.

"See you Saturday, Jules."

"So how have you two been? How are you liking your new city?" I ask while on the road to the 'special park' Saturday morning.

Evie is completely enthralled playing with a magnetic drawing board in the back seat and doesn't answer. Jules shrugs, her shapely shoulders bare in one of Dylan's old cut-off t-shirts. "The summer has been great. The parks are great. It's great being with Callie and Ryan so often. Staying with my dad has been great."

Sure. Sounds like things are really great, I think to myself sarcastically.

"But?" I ask, because I know there's a 'but.'

Jules rakes her fingers through her hair, her tell that she is feeling anything but 'great.' "But it's been a lot of big changes after so many big changes. It's hard meeting other kids for Evie to spend time with, getting to know anyone," Jules admits, her expression unreadable. "I'm hoping once Evie's in school she'll get to make some friends. She's starting soccer in a few weeks, too, so she'll hopefully make some friends from that. And once I'm in school maybe I'll get to make some friends, too," Jules says with a smile that doesn't quite reach her eyes.

Remember when you told her she would have you *for a friend? Way to go, Jake,* I scold myself. "I'm sure you will. Both of you. And now that things are slowing down with my work with the major construction season slowing down, I'll be down to spend more time with you girls, too."

Jules shakes her head with a smile. "Jake, we always love seeing you, but I know you have your own…social life. So, don't worry about us."

Social life? What's that supposed to mean? I wonder to myself. *Is she referring to that whole "flavor-of-the-month" nonsense? I've probably given her plenty of reasons to believe that,* I think sheepishly.

~~~

When I walked into my apartment my jaw dropped in amazement. Jules had completely outdone herself decorating for Dylan's 21st birthday party. The basketball theme was spot on down to the beer pong game setup complete with "nets" and "basketballs" - white plastic cups and orange ping pong balls she had drawn lines on to look like nets and basketballs. Dylan was going to flip when he saw what Jules had done. Where is Jules anyway? *I wondered. My phone lit up with Jules's number.* Speak of the devil, *I grinned to myself.*

"Jules, it looks amazing in here. Dylan is going to love it."

"Oh, so you *are* there. Just thirty minutes later than I asked you to be there," she snapped.

I looked at the clock. Shit.

"I think I already know the answer to this question, but… Did you get the keg?" she asked.

Double shit. *"I'll head out right now and get it," I said already racing back out the door.*

"Don't bother," Jules huffed. "I'm halfway there already." *The line went dead.*

I was waiting on the balcony a half hour later when Jules drove up.

"Well, come on," she shouted up to me. "Get down here and help me carry this stupid keg upstairs."

I raced down the steps and together we carried the keg up the stairs and into the apartment. Jules was surprisingly strong for someone so slender.

"I'm sorry I was late," *I apologized once we had the keg in place.* "A
~~~

friend needed a ride home." Well actually, *your* friend, Rachel, *I added to myself, wincing internally. "And it took longer than I expected."* Because I lost track of time when her face was all over my face, *I remembered, hoping, not for the first time, that Jules couldn't read my thoughts.*

"Whatever. Please just do the only other thing I asked you to do and get me that basketball jersey for me to wear."

"Um..." I mumbled rubbing the back of my neck, thinking about my jersey sitting at the bottom of my laundry pile. Triple shit.

Jules rolled her eyes, knowing, without me having to say it out loud, that she wouldn't be wearing that jersey. "Unbelievable," Jules grumbled pulling out her phone. "I'll borrow one from someone else."

Chagrined, I started down the hall to my room. "Hey, Rachel," I heard Jules say. I stopped in my tracks. Rachel? Fuck. *I slowly turned around facing Jules who was pulling the phone slightly away from her ear; even across the room I heard Rachel's muffled shrieks and giggles on the other end. Jules's face had gone completely blank, like she had had this conversation with other friends too many times before.*

"Oh he gave you a ride? How sweet...And then you what?... Wow, Rachel, how exciting," Jules said almost robotically. "Well you'll have to tell me all about it at the party tonight. Oh and I guess you'll be seeing Jake again then, too. OoOoh," she cooed in a sing-songy voice that I knew, but Rachel probably didn't, was completely fake.

What? Rachel was coming to the party? Double fuck. *"So I was wondering, do you have an extra basketball jersey I can borrow?" Jules asked, undeterred. "Thanks! You just saved the day, Rachel!"*

Jules ended the call then started busying herself with final party preparations as I stood awkwardly in the hallway.

"Jake, you need to tap the keg," Jules ordered, her voice broaching no argument.

"Sure, I can do that," I said, trying to sound completely casual and not like I wanted the floor to swallow me up.

"Done," I said cheerfully when I finished my task. I pointed smiling to the successfully tapped keg, but my smile fell when I saw the way Jules's eyes were narrowed at me.

"What?"

"For once could you just not hook up with one of my friends? Can you just meet someone on your own?"

You're the one dating *my* best friend who you met through *me, I wanted to snap at her. But I bit my tongue, because I knew it wasn't the same. Me casually hooking up with her friends was in no way equivalent to what she and Dylan had.*

I gave her what I hoped was a charming smile. "I can't help it when you have such attractive friends."

Jules blinked at me, her expression unreadable. Then she walked toward the door grabbing her purse on the way. "Everything's set here. I'm going to my place to get ready. I'll be back in an hour. People should get here not too long after me, and Dylan should be here in two. Try not to screw anything up while I'm gone. It's your best friend's birthday, you know." She slammed the door, not even waiting for my reply.

I trudged back to my room and flopped onto my bed covering my face with my pillow. Damn that was bad. Even for me.

~~~

Even though it was years ago, I still feel guilty for some of those lower moments. And I think, somewhat shamefaced, that Jules probably remembers those low moments just as well as, if not better than, I do.

"I think you might have me confused with Jake, your 23-year-old *roomie,*" I say to Jules teasing. "I'm Jake the 28-year-old who spends every Thursday night having dinner with his parents."

"It's nice to hear you're still so close with your parents," Jules says. She doesn't seem to understand that I'm trying to explain that I'm not the same person I was in high school or college. Or maybe she just doesn't buy it. And I guess I can't blame her for that.

When we make the turn into the 'special park' - a state park not too far out of town that has been a favorite of my family's for years - I see a true smile spread across Jules's face. She didn't let on that she knew where we were headed, but the kayak on top of my car was kind of a giveaway. The day use area of this state park has
~~~

everything I had in mind for today. We'll kayak, there's a swimming beach, and I'll even be able to grill hot dogs and we can roast marshmallows at the picnic spot I was able to reserve.

I park the car and we all clamber out of our seats. Evie looks around, her forehead furrowed in confusion. "Where's the slide?" she asks.

I start to feel guilty, like I've somehow misled Evie. I didn't realize to Evie "park" means "playground." Jules sees my worried expression and places a hand on my arm that I'm guessing is to reassure me.

"No slide here, sweet pea. But I think Uncle Jake is taking you out on his kayak. Just remember you have to wear a life jacket."

"I don't have a life jacket," Evie says with a small pout; I have to bite the inside of my cheek not to laugh because that pout absolutely reminds me of Jules. She may look like Dylan, but personality-wise Evie is all Jules.

I step out of the car and open up the back. "No lifejacket? Are you sure?" I ask holding up the purple and pink life jacket I found Wednesday night. Evie's eyes light up and she starts bouncing in place in excitement.

Jules

Evie is a bit pouty when I tell her she has to wear the lifejacket whenever she is in the water – be it on a kayak or just swimming around. Jake is a good sport and tells Evie he will wear his life jacket the whole time, too.

I shrug off my cut-off t-shirt so that I'm just in my one-piece bathing suit and board shorts. I notice Jake staring not too politely, making me feel more than a little self-conscious and like I want to put my t-shirt back on. "What?" I ask, annoyed. Jake looks up at my face, eyes wide with surprise like he didn't realize he was staring.

"Nothing," he says quickly then frowns. I know he has something to say. "It's just, uh…" I raise my hands as if to say *What is it?* He rubs the back of his neck in her nervous way. "It's just you've always been super… athletic, Jules, but you just look really… uh… really thin. Even for you. And I just to want to know if… if you're OK." He looks so embarrassed to be saying this to me, like the last thing he wants to do is comment on my weight. But he also looks so concerned, I'm sure he felt somehow duty-bound to say something.

"I'm fine," I say reflexively. *Let's see how great you would be looking eight months after losing the person you love the most in the world*, I think bitterly. But then I realize it's Jake I'm talking to and that comment would be more than a little tone deaf.

I can tell by the look on Jake's face, that answer wasn't enough. "I exercise a lot in the summer. And we play at parks most days." Jake is still looking at me like he's not buying my answers. I sigh. "And I've been pretty stressed for the past… oh… *year* or so," I admit, and Jake gives me a small half-smile, nodding in understanding. "But it's not something you should worry about."

"I'm allowed to worry about you, Jules," Jake says defensively.

"Why? Because of some ridiculous notion that you owe it to Dylan to take care of me?" I snap.

"No. Not because of Dylan," Jake responds, his voice slow and measured. "Because I'm your friend, Jules. And I have been for a long time."

I run my hands through my hair and make a small nod of concession. He's right. He's my friend, and I shouldn't be upset with him for worrying about me.

"Thank you for looking out for me. I really am fine. So please don't worry. OK?"

He nods, still eyeing me warily, but letting the subject drop. At least for now.

It is so much fun watching Jake and Evie playing together. Evie is in heaven riding with Jake in his kayak then playing in the swimming area with him. Jake is really just a big kid at heart, so he comes up with the most hilarious games for him and Evie to play in the water. He has also splashed me at least a half-dozen times, even though I'm not part of the game and I'm just trying to float around and enjoy myself. And each time I splash him back it just seems to encourage him to splash me more. Like I said, a big kid. A big 28-year-old kid.

Jake

It's late afternoon by the time I pull up to Jules's house. Evie is passed out in the back seat, her cheeks and nose pink despite Jules's valiant efforts to apply and reapply and reapply sunscreen. I don't think any amount of sunscreen would protect that fair, freckly skin.

Just like Dylan, I think to myself, remembering an unfortunate sunburn Dylan acquired during a river float before sophomore year. The tops of his feet were scorched; it was the only area of his skin that he had somehow forgotten to protect with sunscreen or clothing. He couldn't wear shoes for a week.

Jules looks pretty worn out herself. But she's smiling at me, and that smile is actually reaching her eyes this time. She unbuckles and steps out of the car silently, then opens Evie's car door. "Wait, let me," I whisper over the top of the car. Jules nods and takes a step back. I hustle over to Evie's door and unbuckle her. As I lift Evie from the car, she mumbles some garbled complaint but allows me to wrap her arms around my neck. Wordlessly, I follow Jules into the house, up the stairs, to Evie's room. I place Evie onto her bed as gently as possible. Before I go, I place a kiss on Evie's forehead. She rolls over, and I dart from her room, afraid I've woken her up.

Jules cracks up silently in the hallway, and I give her a light, indignant shove as I pass her. She walks back out to the car with me to gather their things. I carry Evie's backpack to the door.

"Thank you for giving up your Saturday for us, Jake. I think Evie is going to be asking to go kayaking with Uncle Jake every day for the next six months."

"She can come kayaking with me any time. And I wasn't 'giving up' my Saturday, Jules," I explain, again, trying not to sound annoyed. "I've been working so much, this was by far the best Saturday I've had all summer." Jules does not look at all convinced. "Hanging with Evie is always a blast. And you can be fun, too," I add with a grin because I can't pass up a chance to rile up Jules. She shoves me in the shoulder, making me grin ever wider.

"Just you wait, Jules. You'll be spending so much time with me you'll be sick of me," I call to her as I walk back to my car.

"Who says I'm not already sick of you?" she calls back but with a grin that lets me know she's just kidding. At least I think so. "See you soon, Jake."

CHAPTER 5

Jake

I spot Jules sitting on the hood of her car, wrapped up in an over-sized fleece jacket that I recognize as Dylan's. She is watching Evie's soccer practice - or I guess you call a bunch of four- and five-year-olds running around playing silly games that involve a soccer ball a *practice*. Jules sees me approach.

"What are you doing here?" she asks and gives me a wan smile as I hand her the coffee I picked up for her on the way over.

Trying to be your friend. Trying to support you and my goddaughter, if you'll let me, I plead internally. "Bringing you what looks like some much-needed caffeine and watching a quality live sporting event," I say gesturing to the cute chaos happening on the soccer field.

Evie is running around in a circular path with a few other kids yelling, "Flying unicorn!"

"You look absolutely beat," I say to Jules as I sit down on the car hood next to her. *You also look like I should have bought you a dozen donuts to go with that coffee,* I think noticing again how thin she looks.

Jules lets her head fall back dramatically. "Oh my God, kindergarteners are exhausting," she grumbles. "I had students this week who legitimately did not understand how to sit cross-legged on the carpet. I had to demonstrate and bend their legs the right way for them. How did they not know that? And trying to line them up to walk in the hallway? Herding cats. Herding cats."

I chuckle. "Did Ms. Nelson have a hard week? Oh shoot I mean Mrs. Bailey," I say wincing. Old habits are hard to break and I've never adjusted to her taking Dylan's last name.

"No, Nelson's right. Never changed my name at work, and never even changed it legally," she sighs with a weak smile.

"So kindergarten is going about how you expected?" I ask trying to move quickly past my blunder.

"I don't know what I expected, but I don't think anything could have prepared me for the first week of kindergarten."

"Not a forever job, I'm guessing?"

Jules takes a gulp of coffee. "No, definitely not. I'm so grateful to have this job, to be at this school. Evie will go there next year, which will be so convenient and just a dream to work at her school. And it's great working in the same building as Sarah. But teaching kindergarten is already kicking my butt. If there's an option to switch grade levels next year I'm jumping on it. Enough about my job," she says abruptly changing the subject. "How are things at work for my second favorite architect?"

"Second favorite?" I ask a bit miffed. "Who's your favorite?"

"Your dad of course," Jules says with a teasing smile. I roll my eyes. Of course she would say that. My dad has been completely charmed by Jules since we were twelve; she asked to play his guitar, sang him a little song about love and rainbows, and he was a goner.

"Things are great. This community is booming, so we're busier than ever. We're thinking about bringing a third architect on." It's been just the two of us for the past few years, but my dad's looking ahead to retirement in a few years, and we're figuring out what the road ahead might look like for JT Architects.

"Do you think you'll always teach?" I ask Jules. My mom is a 30-plus-year teacher, but I know it's not for everyone.

Jules shrugs. "My last principal was encouraging me to get a license to become a principal."

"Being so bossy is helpful when you're the boss," I say with a grin. "Why don't you do that? Get that license?"

Jules purses her lips. "I was going to. Dylan and I had a plan for it. I was going to start courses last fall, but then… all plans went to shit." She sighs. "And now working full-time and parenting on my own I just don't see how I could do school work on top of everything."

"Don't give up on it completely. Maybe now isn't the time, but I think you should reconsider it later, when you're more settled into your new job and you and Evie get into a more established routine. Principal Nelson has a nice ring to it," I say elbowing Jules.

"Maybe," Jules says not sounding too convinced.

"Well when you do decide, there are a lot of people, me included, who would want to help take some of the load off of you." She nods, and I decide to drop the subject. For now. "How was Evie's first week of school?" I ask.

Jules rakes her fingers through her hair in her anxious way, making me nervous that something must have gone wrong at Evie's school. "Her teacher told me she didn't say a word. Not one word. The entire week."

"The kid out there yelling 'Flying unicorn' didn't say a word at school?" I ask incredulously.

Jules laughs. "She's only doing that because she likes her coach," Jules says pointing at the tall blond that all of the kids are running around, like the sun of their chaotic solar system.

I take my sunglasses off. "Oh wow that's Callie! I didn't even notice!" *Good on Callie. She must really love kids to* volunteer *for this mayhem.*

"Exactly. Evie will talk to me, my dad, Callie, sometimes Ryan, and you. That's it."

I am surprised and strangely proud that I'm one of the few people on Evie's worthy-of-verbal-communication list.

"Was that a problem at her last school?" I ask.

"No, it was one of the places she felt secure and comfortable after… after Dylan," Jules responds.

"I'm sure she just needs time to get comfortable in her new

school," I say, trying to sound positive when my heart is aching for sweet Evie. "And soon she'll be jabbering their ears off. Just like her mom," I add just to get a rise out of Jules. She shoves me. Then she's shaking her head, unsmiling.

"This is all so hard on her. And I feel so helpless," she says quietly. "Like there's nothing I can do to make it easier on her."

"You *are* making things easier on her. And you have to give yourself some credit, because you're doing such an amazing job when it's all pretty hard on you, too, Jules."

"I'm fine," she says automatically; I know not to push the subject, even though I'm aware that her answer wasn't completely honest. We sip our coffees silently, enjoying watching the pack of children chase Callie across the field. I *think* that's the point of the game they are playing, but I'm not sure.

Jules lets out a long breath. "Being a single parent sucks," she admits. "I know how hard it was on my dad being a single parent. And I always told myself my kids would have both parents. But here I am raising my kid alone," she sighs.

"That's not anyone's fault, Jules," I say gently.

"I know that. It's not like anyone *chose* to leave in this case," Jules says frowning. I don't know much about Jules and Callie's mom; Jules never mentioned her growing up and I never had the courage to ask. Dylan told me once that she left when Jules was really young. Even with a great father like Robert, that experience can still take its toll.

Jules

It's been so long since she was part of my life, sometimes I forget that I ever even had a mom. My mom and dad met in college, both students at UCLA. When they graduated my dad found a job with the Oregon Department of Transportation, and they struck out for Bend, Oregon - a city that was starting to really boom and was drawing a lot of California transplants. They quickly had Callie, followed shortly by me.

Within a few years my mom made it clear that she was miserable. She blamed the central Oregon weather, the small town feel of the city, the isolation of central Oregon. In an effort to make my mom happy, my dad applied for a job with the California Department of Transportation, and we moved to the LA area. Perfect weather, completely urban – it was exactly what my mom said she wanted. We were there for a few years, and I think for a while there was hope that the move would keep our family together.

But as it turned out it wasn't the location that had been making my mom miserable. It was being a wife and mom. We could be in Bend, LA, Brooklyn, or Louisiana - she would hate it anywhere. Before I was five years old, she left us. I don't even know where she went.

My dad packed up Callie and me and brought us back to Bend just as I was entering elementary school. For a while we would get an occasional phone call and a yearly birthday card from our mom, but even that stopped after a few years. Callie and I haven't heard from her since we were kids, and I have no desire to ever hear from her again. As far as I'm concerned, my family is better off without her.

Even though my dad did an incredible job as a single parent, it wasn't always easy for him, Callie, or me. I always told myself that if I had kids they would have two parents. Probably everyone thinks that when they plan for the future, and I was so naïve to think I had that kind of control over my life. But Dylan's illness completely changed the equation. Fuck cancer.

Jake

Jules is quiet for a long time, which in the past was highly unusual for her but I've noticed happening more frequently since January. I feel myself squirming in the discomfort of the unexpected silence.

"You're quiet," I say to Jules eventually, unable to bear her silence, 'You're quiet' is something I'm positive I've never said to her before.

"I know," she says with a shy smile. "Just thinking."

"What are you thinking?" I ask, nudging her with my elbow.

She shakes her head again. "I just feel like I am completely failing at this single mom gig," she admits. "And I have so much help!" she moans, covering her face with her hands.

I'm stunned by her confession. "Failing?" I say incredulously. I pull her hands from her face, so that she can't ignore or hide from what I say. "You are doing an incredible job, Jules. Evie is doing great. Just look at her. She is thriving, which I don't think anyone would have expected under the circumstances."

Jules purses her lips. "I just almost feel guilty depending on everyone. My dad, Callie, *you*," she says gesturing at me with dismay. "And I don't know how my dad did it on his own. Two kids. By himself. No family. How did he do it?"

"Your dad is incredible, and he did what he had to do. I know you would be doing great all on your own, too. But you don't have to because you have people around you who love you and want to support you. I don't think that having help from your family and friends is something you should feel guilty about, Jules. Having a whole team of people who are there to help raise your kid is a great thing, something a lot of people would aspire to have. Isn't that something every kid would want? A whole crew just to love and admire them?"

Jules gives me a sidelong look. "Yeah, Evie does have a pretty great crew," she says with a genuine smile that makes me feel like a million bucks.

Suddenly a head of wild, dark, curly hair is bobbing in front of me. "Come prance, Uncle Jake!" Evie orders, grabbing my hand and pulling me off of the hood of the car.

"I thought this was soccer," I say helplessly as she drags me to the field.

"No. We're flying unicorns," she says adamantly. "Come!"

Jules just grins and waves as she watches Evie lead me in my first ever attempt to *prance.*

"Do I look as majestic as I feel?" I call to Jules.

"Absolutely, Unicorn King," she calls back.

CHAPTER 6

Jules

Evie is bouncing in her seat, wound up with anticipation. I can barely manage to get her to eat a few bites of toast between her shrieks of excitement and her requests of "Can we go out now?" at regular, ten-second intervals. It is 6AM on a Saturday and she has been up since five bouncing around like a bunny on caffeine.

"Just a few more minutes. We need to have a good breakfast so we have enough energy to play," I explain. *And Mommy needs a week's worth of coffee to have enough energy for this,* I mutter to myself.

As I finish my last bite of toast, Evie asks, once again, "Can we go out now?"

I drain the last of my coffee. "Yes, we can go out now," I answer smiling but groaning a bit inwardly. "Let's go find your snow suit." Evie dashes to the garage where her new snow suit is hanging on a hook next to her snow boots, hat, and gloves. Thank goodness we went shopping for winter gear a few weeks ago.

It's the first snow of the season and Evie is over the moon excited about playing in the snow in her own front yard. When we lived in Eugene, snow was rare and we only went on excursions to snowy parts of the state a few times a season. Now that we live in Central

Oregon, snow will be a constant for the next few months. I feel grouchy just thinking about having to scrape ice off of my windshield for the next five-plus months.

I sigh inwardly as I pull on my own snow pants and boots, feeling that it is too early for this kind of activity on a Saturday. But as we step out of the door, I feel myself fall under the snow's spell. I watch Evie's eyes grow wide and her mouth form a silent O as she takes in the winter wonderland that less than 12 hours ago was an unremarkable suburban street. There's something truly magical about the first snow of the season. Seeing this snowy miracle through Evie's eyes I am reminded of that and grateful to be with her sharing this special morning. The caffeine kicking in also might be helping elevate my mood.

I watch as Evie looks back and forth between her snow boots and the untouched snow, as if she's afraid to ruin it. I feel a mischievous grin spread across my face. I drop Evie's hand and take off running – or shuffling as quickly as I can manage in all of my snow gear – then spin and plop heavily on my back onto the snow-covered lawn. I hear Evie giggle, and I lift my head to watch her run and plop, mimicking my own movements.

While Evie and I are laying on our backs giggling and making snow angels I hear a pair of boots crunching on the snow-covered lawn. I assume it must be my dad coming to see what we're up to.

Evie squeals, "We're making snow angels!"

"How are you making snow angels when you two are already snow angels?" a familiar voice asks. My breath catches in my throat. *Not my dad,* I realize, my face burning, as I stare up into Jake's smiling face, his dark eyes sparkling with amusement.

"Hi," I say quietly, still lying on the snow, arms and legs spread out like a starfish. Jake grins at me and reaches a hand down to help me up. "What are you doing here?" I ask as he easily pulls me to standing.

"When I woke up I looked in my fridge and found this," he says pulling a large, orange carrot out of his jacket pocket. "And I thought it would be the perfect nose for a snowman. What do you think, Evie? Can you help me build a snowman?"

"Yes!" Evie shrieks snatching the carrot then grabbing Jake's leg in a fierce hug. They spend the next half hour building a wonderfully lumpy, misshapen snowman, complete with carrot nose.

More snow angels are followed by a very adorable snowball fight in which Jake misses Evie every time but somehow manages to hit me at least a dozen times. With my awful throwing skills, I barely land a hit. I can tell by the way Evie is shivering she needs a break to warm up. She will not admit that she is cold even though she is shaking like a leaf. I finally entice her to come inside with a promise of hot chocolate.

"Coffee or hot chocolate for you?" I ask Jake.

"For me?" he asks with a surprised look.

I nod at him. "Yes, for you."

"Um, both?" he asks with a small grin.

I shake my head laughing. "Both it is." And we all head inside to warm up.

Jake

The three of us are huddled around the fireplace enjoying our cups of hot chocolate and coffee (or one cup of each in my case) when Robert walks into the living room.

"Morning girls," he says in his low, gruff voice. When his eyes land on me I see him pull up short. "Jacob," he says with an edge to his voice. I notice him glance at the clock. It's only 8AM. "When did you get here?" he asks gruffly, his eyes narrowed at me. I've always had a feeling Robert didn't like me, and seeing me in his living room so early in the morning seems to strike a nerve.

"We made a snowman, Bobpa!" Evie calls excitedly. "I'll show you!" Evie runs over and beckons her grandfather to the front door to admire her snowman. "Uncle Jake gived us the carrot!" Evie says in her perfectly adorable five-year-old way.

"Well wasn't that nice of Jacob," Robert says coolly.

"Coffee, Dad?" Jules asks, striding toward the kitchen, pushing up the sleeves of her over-sized t-shirt that I recognize as Dylan's. Robert grunts his assent, and Jules beckons me to follow her.

"Sorry. He's not much of a morning person," she whispers ruefully as she pours a cup for her dad and a refill for me. I have a sneaking suspicion that Robert would be displeased to see me no matter the time of day.

After I finish my (two) mugs, I load all of our mugs into the dishwasher.

"You didn't have to do that," Jules says apologetically.

"Easy," I say, shrugging, trying not to be annoyed that accepting my help, even something so small as loading five mugs into a dishwasher, is still difficult for her.

I start putting on my jacket to go. "You're leaving?" Evie asks, with huge, sad eyes. "But I want another snowball fight!"

"I know, sweet pea, but I'm worried if I have another snowball fight with your mom I'll end up with another black eye," I say winking at Jules. Her eyeballs roll to the heavens.

"I thought I might actually make it through one snowy day without you bringing that up," she laments, making me grin.

~~~

On a Saturday early in the snowy season of our freshman year of high school, several of our friends met up at our old elementary school. The little hill behind the school served as a perfect sledding slope. After we had our fill of sledding we walked through the playground on our way home. As the story goes, somehow a spontaneous snowball fight erupted. I always said somehow *when really I knew the infamous snowball fight started with me throwing a snowball at Jules's back when she was walking in front of me. Her lime green ski jacket was calling to me, just begging to be hit by a snowball. I had no choice; the snowball hit its target with a satisfying* whack. *When Jules turned to glare at me, a snowball landed on my right arm. I looked to see our friend Danny grinning at me then tossing another snowball that hit me in the side of the face. In an instant, snowballs were flying in every direction.*

A few minutes into the snowball fight, I was smirking to myself triumphantly after landing a perfect toss squarely on Danny's head. I was startled by Jules standing only a few feet away from me with a snowball
~~~

in each hand. She had an evil grin on her face, poised for payback for hitting her from behind without cause. Jules couldn't throw worth a darn, so I knew I wasn't in any danger. But just to be funny I turned and ran, trying to get away from her. I saw one snowball sail past me.

I turned my head laughing and yelled, "Missed!" while still running full speed.

"Jake, watch out!" I heard Jules scream a moment before my face connected with the playground's tetherball pole.

I sported a black eye for the next week and made sure everyone knew it was all Jules's fault.

~~~

Every time it snows I retell that story - leaving out the parts about me starting the snowball fight and me turning around while I ran - placing all of the blame on Jules for chasing me directly into the pole and giving me a black eye. I have always known it was my own fault for being such an idiot and not looking where I was going. But if I told the whole truth and nothing but the truth, then I wouldn't get to blame Jules. And what's the fun in that? And every time I tell my version of the story Jules rolls her eyes to the sky like she is praying for more patience or the strength to stop herself from wringing my neck. The same way she's rolling her eyes right now.

I kneel down to Evie's eye level. "I can't stay because I have to head into work," I explain gently to Evie. I only stopped by to leave the carrot as a surprise for them to find on their doorstep while I was on my way to a building site that is behind schedule. To my delight I stumbled upon Jules and Evie already playing in the snow and couldn't pass up a chance to play. That kid must wake up *early*.

"I'm sorry I can't stay, sweet pea. We will have lots of chances to have snowball fights this winter, don't you worry. And I bet your mom and grandfather would love to have a snowball fight with you," I say avoiding any eye contact with Robert.

"OK," Evie says, sadly, giving me a pathetic little hug.

"Make sure you keep an eye on that snowman," I tell her in a
~~~

secretive whisper. "You never know what he might get up to when you're not looking."

Evie's eyes sparkle with excitement. Jules is standing by the entryway watching our exchange. She shakes her head at me with a small grin on her face, then she follows me out the door.

"Thank you for this fun surprise. You're too good to us." I don't know what to say in response to her undeserved praise, so I just smile at her awkwardly. "That's rough having to work on the weekend," Jules continues. "But I think you're actually getting off easy. I'm sure Evie will drag me out here at least six more times today." She makes small mock-crying sounds, and I roll my eyes.

"How about you visit the building site and I stay here to have another snowball fight," I offer, teasingly.

"Gladly," Jules deadpans.

"Keep an eye on that snowman," I say as I ruffle her hair and turn to leave.

She bats my hand away playfully. "Hey wait, Jake," she says grabbing my arm, and I turn back to look at her, my eyes lingering on her hand on my arm. "I've been meaning to ask you, does your family have plans for Thanksgiving?"

"Yeah, actually my parents are heading to Washington to see my aunt and uncle."

"Oh, darn. I was hoping you all would join us," she says looking crestfallen.

"But *I* don't have any plans," I clarify. I love my parents, but six hours one-way in the back seat of their car just did not appeal to me this year.

"Really?" she says brightly. "OK, good. Then it's settled. You'll have Thanksgiving with us."

It's settled? I don't remember saying yes, I laugh to myself.

"Who's us?" I ask skeptically.

Jules starts ticking off guests, counting on her fingers. "Callie and Ryan, the Baileys - Dylan's mom and dad, Laurel and her fiancé," I frown thinking about spending a holiday with Dylan's sister who neither Jules nor I have ever gotten along with very well. Truthfully, Dylan didn't get along with her that well, either. "And then Evie, my dad, and me," Jules continues. "And you of course make ten. I was hoping for an even dozen with your folks but ten will be perfect."

Ten people? Part of me wants to say no and just make myself an awesome turkey sandwich and watch football, but seeing the hopeful look on Jules's face I just can't say no.

"Sure, Jules, that sounds wonderful. Let me know what I can bring."

"Just yourself," Jules says, with a mega-watt smile that will warm me for the rest of the day.

CHAPTER 7

Jake

The Nelsons' front door is unlocked so I walk in without knocking. I knew there would be a lot of people at this Thanksgiving gathering, but seeing everyone in person is a bit overwhelming. I typically spend Thanksgiving with just my parents, so ten people feels like a lot. Dylan's parents, his older sister, Laurel, and her fiancé, Ian, Callie, Ryan, Robert, and Evie are all in the living room enjoying some appetizers. I take a few minutes saying hello to everyone, half-wishing I were at home enjoying a turkey sandwich.

Part-way through my hellos Evie hops off of Callie's lap, runs over, and gives me a tight squeeze that fills my heart.

"Come give Grandma one of those hugs," Dylan's mom calls to Evie from across the room, her arms outstretched. Evie runs in the other direction reclaiming her place on her aunt's lap and nuzzling into Callie, who beams at Evie's sweet affection and plants a kiss on Evie's curly head. I see Dylan's mom purse her lips in annoyance.

I look over to the kitchen and spot Jules alone in the kitchen flitting around the room like a humming bird. She looks great in a simple burgundy dress with her hair pulled back in some twisty style. She is definitely looking healthier than she did this summer, more like her normally fit and athletic self, and I'm hoping that means she's feeling less stressed these days. But I don't dare say anything, because I'm not a complete idiot. I know that any iteration of 'You look like you've gained some much-needed weight' would not be received well no matter how well-intentioned or accurate.

I stand in the doorway and spot a cutting board next to a stack of washed vegetables that need to be chopped. "Hey, Jules," I say as I walk over to the sink to wash my hands.

"Oh! Hey, Jake," she responds, looking a bit startled. "Sorry I didn't see you come in."

I walk over to the cutting board and start chopping.

"You don't have to do that," Jules insists, looking alarmed.

Will you just let me help you for once! I want to roar at her. "I want to," I say as cheerfully as I can manage.

Jules stops short and looks at me. "OK, thank you," she says, and I think she actually means it. "When you finish that I have another job for you," she says as she returns to flitting about the kitchen. *Of course, you do*, I think; it takes all my self-control not to smirk at her.

Jules

I don't dare admit it, but I am grateful for Jake's help. Before he walked into the kitchen I was so overwhelmed I was certain we wouldn't be eating dinner until midnight. I had what I thought was a pretty good plan for the day, divvying out the responsibility for many of the side dishes and desserts between Callie and Ryan and the members of the Bailey family. Callie and Ryan came through with what I asked them to bring, but Ellen called the night before asking if she could just bring a cheese platter as an appetizer and Laurel texted me that she wasn't sure what she would bring yet. So that meant four dishes that I hadn't planned to make myself were suddenly on my already busy to-do list.

Jake takes over some of those added responsibilities, taking some of the load off of me, which I more than appreciate. He doesn't even tease me about always telling him what to do like he normally would. He has me laughing so much as we work, I feel far more relaxed and like I'm actually enjoying the day, which was not the case before he arrived.

Jake

Eventually other guests come into the kitchen making feeble offers to help, but mostly asking Jules to help *them*. There are several moments when Jules looks a little overwhelmed; people keep asking her for direction while she's in the middle of something or in the middle of twelve things at once. I want to say *'Figure it out yourself'* at least a dozen times on Jules's behalf, but she always answers politely with clear direction; she takes multi-tasking to a whole new level and runs the entire show with poise and grace. But even Jules has her limits, and I see a fire building in her eyes that has me on edge.

"I think we're just about ready," Jules says proudly after she lays the last dish on the buffet in the dining room. I look up from the turkey drawings Evie and I have been making in the living room, awed by the feast Jules has made for us. I notice Jules staring at the oven, eyes wide with surprise. She dashes over and quickly opens the oven door. She pulls out a tray of rolls that someone must have stuffed in the oven then forgotten about not too long ago.

"Oh no! My rolls look burned!" Laurel wails from the doorway. "Did you not set the timer?" she asks Jules with more than a hint of reproach in her voice.

What? When she was busy preparing every other dish for this giant meal, she was supposed to set a timer for your *rolls?* I growl to myself. Laurel has some nerve. Jules looks like she is about to scream. Instead she purses her lips and sets the pan of slightly burned rolls down. Then she tosses her oven mitts on the counter, opens the sliding door to the back porch, and walks out of the house.

The entire roomful of guests stares silently at the sliding door. Everyone glances around nervously. Without Jules to direct the show, no one seems to know what to do.

"Callie, you'd better go check on your sister," I hear Robert say in his low, gruff voice.

Callie starts toward the door, but I'm closer. I hold my hand up, stopping Callie in her tracks. "You stay, Callie. I'll check on her," I offer, already opening the door.

I step out onto the back porch and close the sliding door behind me. Jules hasn't gone far; she's sitting on the step that leads to the back yard. She doesn't turn or acknowledge me as I walk over and sit down beside her.

"I thought he would have sent Callie," she mutters, eyes still trained on the steps in front of her.

"That was his first choice, but I volunteered," I say, laying my blazer across her shoulders; she is already shivering in the thin dress she is wearing. Jules pulls my jacket tighter and nods her thanks. We sit quietly for a moment before I ask, "Are you OK?"

She shakes her head, taking a deep breath. "I had to leave before I said anything I would regret. I don't know what I was thinking inviting so many people. Too much pressure. I completely cracked under it."

"No, you didn't, Jules," I scoff. "One set of slightly burned rolls is nothing when you're putting together a holiday meal for ten people. And those rolls weren't even your responsibility." I would like to ream that spoiled brat Laurel for placing the blame on Jules.

"It's not the rolls," Jules mutters.

"I kind of figured that out," I say softly. I bump her shoulder with my own. "So what is it?"

She sighs and rakes her fingers through her hair. "It just feels like ever since Dylan, I'm responsible for everyone else's happiness. And sometimes it's just too much."

My jaw drops. It takes me a second to respond to her outrageous idea. "How are you responsible for everyone else's happiness?" I ask, flabbergasted.

"That's how it feels," she snaps defensively. "Like today. I'm walking this horrible tightrope where everyone wants to know that I'm happy, that Evie's happy, that we're doing well. But also they want to hear that we're miserable and nothing is great without Dylan. Because if we're not at least a little miserable then maybe I didn't cherish Dylan enough, maybe I don't miss him enough. But if we're too miserable nobody wants to hear it because that would just be too hard for anyone else to handle.

"And Dylan's family, they just want Evie to be this performing little doll who just makes everyone else feel better, but she's a person with her own feelings and moods. And she can't always just light up everyone's day. And she barely sees them. How do they expect her to be comfortable with them when she hasn't seen them in months?

"And for God's sake why am I responsible for setting a timer for everyone's stupid dish. Can't anyone figure out how to set their own timer? Everyone in that room above the age of five has their own cell phone. Set your own God damn timer!"

Jules buries her face in her hands, and I'm worried she might be crying. And I don't know how I'll handle it if she's crying, because in eighteen years I've *never* seen her cry. Not once. But then, to my relief and bewilderment, I realize she's laughing. "God I wish those rolls had burned to ash just to see the look on Laurel's face." We both laugh; neither of us have ever been Laurel fans and seeing her react to her rolls being completely ruined might have been worth it.

~~~

Jules and Dylan had been seeing each other for a few months, when Dylan invited Jules and me to drive up to Corvallis to meet his sister, Laurel, a senior at Oregon State. On the drive up from Eugene I could tell Jules was nervous to be meeting Dylan's sister for the first time. She was jabbering away as usual telling endless stories about funny things that happened in her classes, but she seemed almost flighty, like a hummingbird ready to dart away at any moment. Dylan just listened, smiling, completely enthralled. This first meeting was actually a pretty big deal for Jules; Dylan was her first boyfriend and he was introducing her to his only sister. I knew it was a big deal to Dylan, too. Even though he had dated some in high school, Jules was his first serious girlfriend.

It ended up being an incredibly disappointing evening; Laurel was
~~~

incredibly rude to both Jules and me from the very moment we met. Laurel took one look at me, taking in my lacrosse team sweatshirt and U of O ballcap and judged me to be an idiot meathead. She regarded me as if she thought I was plain stupid. Worse yet, her whole demeanor, the comments that she made, everything in that first meeting made it so painfully obvious she didn't think Jules was good enough for Dylan. And if Jules wasn't good enough for Dylan in Laurel's eyes, no one would ever be good enough for her baby brother.

Once we were seated, Dylan asked Laurel, "How is LSAT prep coming along?"

Laurel sighed loudly. "It's a lot on top of an already busy senior year. My test date is next month. I'm sure it will be fine and then I can concentrate on law school applications. So are you still planning to major in math, Dyl?"

"Yeah, that's the plan. And then I'm thinking maybe a master's in education so I can teach," Dylan said, with a smile directed at Jules.

"What?!" Laurel shrieked. "Teach? No, Dyl, absolutely not." We all stared at her, shocked by her outburst. "That is so beneath you," she exclaimed, glancing far too obviously at Jules.

"What's wrong with teaching?" Jules asked calmly, but having known her for so long I could tell she was barely containing her rage; she was also planning to earn a master's in education after completing a psychology degree.

"I mean, there's nothing wrong with teaching. For some people," Laurel said, glancing at me, like she thought such a lowly position might suit the idiot, jock roommate. "But Dylan is so bright, top of his class in high school. He should just be doing something…better." What a thing to say in front of two prospective teachers and the son of a career teacher.

"Like what?" Jules, the top of our high school class and a prospective teacher, asked patiently.

"I don't know. Something more … impressive," Laurel explained.

"Like architecture?" I asked.

"Yes. Exactly. Something like architecture," Laurel said in full agreement with the idiot, jock roommate, architecture student. I had to bite my cheek to stop myself from laughing, and I could tell Jules and Dylan were about to crack up, enjoying my joke at Laurel's expense.

When the server came to the table, he had a small grin on his face. "Let me guess," he said tapping his chin thoughtfully. "Siblings," he said pointing at Dylan and Laurel. They both chuckled in a way that made it obvious this scene had played out many times before. They did look a lot alike – dark wavy hair, bright blue eyes, thin, tall. They were clearly related. Then the waiter pointed to Jules and me. "And siblings," he said with a smile. My face fell and Jules blanched. Both curly headed blonds with brown eyes, his mistake was understandable, but being mistaken for Jules's brother felt so…uncomfortable.

After a long, awkward pause, I gave a forced laugh and said, "Nope, not siblings. Just friends."

Jules also gave a shaky laugh. I glanced at Dylan, whose forehead wrinkled slightly, but he didn't say anything. I noticed him take Jules's hand, and she smiled at him so brightly any discomfort for either of them was instantly forgotten. The server left after taking our orders looking a bit chagrined.

"But really, Dyl," Laurel continued. "Teaching? Just no."

Even though Dylan loved teaching and was incredibly happy and successful in his field, Laurel always seemed to blame Jules for leading Dylan into a field that she felt was beneath him. And she made it pretty clear from the start that she didn't just think teaching was beneath him.

~~~

When we stop laughing I see the tension return to Jules's face. I hate seeing her like this. I react without thinking and wrap my arm around her shoulders. She leans in, and I feel her relax into me.

"You are doing an incredible job, and I'm not just talking about this masterpiece of a holiday meal you are somehow pulling off." Jules offers me a half-smile. "And I think everyone is just so amazed by what you are capable of that they take for granted that everything you do, everything you do for *everyone else*, can take its toll. You are not responsible for anyone but yourself and your daughter. Everyone else can set their own damn timers and Laurel can take those rolls and shove them up her…"
~~~

"OK, OK," Jules says, cutting me off, shoving me softly as she sits up straight. "Thank you."

She moves to stand, but I grab her arm lightly to stop her. "And just for the record, even though it's not your responsibility in the least, you and your daughter make everyone here tonight very happy. Everyone," I say earnestly. She smiles shyly at me. "Even with all those feelings and moods you two have," I add with a wink.

Jules makes a small gasp of outrage. "I do not have moods!" she insists.

"Evie gets it from somewhere, and it's not Dylan," I say teasingly. That guy was never in a bad mood in his life. Jules scowls at me. I stand up and extend my hand to her. She takes my hand and I help her stand up.

Once she's on her feet she gently wraps her arms around me. Even though I just had my arm around her, I don't know how to react. *Jules hugging me? That hasn't happened in years.*

"I'm glad you're here," she mumbles into my shoulder, as I awkwardly pat her back.

"Me, too," I say, surprised that I honestly am glad I'm here. "Now let's get inside, because I don't think anyone knows what to do without you. They are probably all still standing exactly where you left them. We are all sheep lost without our shepherd."

"I doubt that," Jules says laughing, handing me my jacket. But as we walk in the door everyone is still in almost exactly the same position they were in when Jules left. She looks at me wide-eyed and I have to bite the inside of my cheek so I don't crack up.

"Well I think that was the last thing to come out of the oven," Jules says to the group. "So let's eat!" Everyone files into the dining room.

I follow Jules into the dining room and whisper in her ear, "Baa."

Jules burst out laughing but quickly covers her mouth. She elbows me in the ribs, which makes me grin even wider. *I'm really glad I'm here.*

CHAPTER 8

Jake

I'm in line at the grocery store when something in the display at the end of the aisle catches my eye. It's early December, so all of the Christmas displays have been up for a few weeks, but this one actually catches my attention. It has winter-themed coloring books and art supplies to go with them.

It takes me about two seconds to decide Evie *needs* a new coloring book and markers and a few sparkly gel pens, too. I also decide Evie *needs* her new art supplies as soon as possible. I call Jules to see if I can drop off my little impromptu, *just because* present.

"Hello?" Jules answers, sounding out of breath.

"Hey sorry to bother you, are you working out or something?"

"No," she says, still sounding winded.

"OK..." I respond slowly. "Is this a bad time?"

"No. Why did you call, Jake?" she asks, her voice clipped.

"I just have something for Evie and I was wondering if now would be an OK time to drop it off."

"Sure. I'll leave the door unlocked," she says hanging up before I can even respond.

That was weird.

I walk into the house and find Evie watching a movie. She magnanimously pauses the movie to open her present. She oohs and aahs over the new art supplies and even gives me a big hug of thanks. But even in the face of a stack of new art supplies, the show must go on. She restarts her movie, instantly ignoring me.

"Where's your mom?" I ask Evie, more than a little surprised I haven't seen Jules yet. She shrugs, attention still fully on her movie.

"In here!" I hear Jules call, and I follow her voice to the garage.

"What is all this?" I ask, eyes wide as I take in the garage. Jules is standing in the middle of a sea of bright blue bags, stuffed with bottles and cans. And it stinks. Really stinks. Like the dumpster behind a bar stinks.

Jules is nervously pushing up and pulling down the sleeves of her over-sized long sleeve shirt that must be Dylan's. "I got roped into being in charge of the bottle drive fundraiser for Evie's school. And now I have to get all of these bags to the bottle drop," she explains, eyes roaming around the garage, clearly overwhelmed by the size of this task.

"Jules, if you would just ask, I would do that for you," I say, already formulating a plan to borrow our company pick-up so that I can load it up and take the bags of cans and bottles to the bottle drop.

"I can't ask you to do that," she says, looking away from me, her voice colder than usual.

"Why not? Why can't you just ask me to help you?" *What is so wrong with asking for my help?*

She shrugs. "It's just easier to do it myself," she replies, busying herself with tying bags.

"No, actually, it's not," I say trying to keep my temper in check. "That's why you ask for help. To make things easier on yourself. To let someone else carry some of the load for you."

"Well it's easier for *me*," she mutters.

"How?" I ask, not letting the subject drop even though I know she wants me to.

"Because then you can't disappoint me!" she snaps, whirling on me. "I have been let down enough. Do you have any idea how that feels? To be depending on someone to have them just drop you like you don't matter? I hate it! And I would rather do it all myself than take the chance that I'll end up regretting ever asking for your help in the first place."

I stare at her, shocked by her outburst. "Disappoint you?" *Like she doesn't matter? How can she think that when she matters so much to me?* "Do you mean everyone in general disappoints you, or me specifically?" I ask, afraid to hear her answer.

She rakes her fingers through her hair in exasperation. "Everyone in general," she grumbles, busying herself again with tying the bags. Her voice lowers as she mutters, "And maybe you specifically, too."

~~~

I tossed about in my bed wanting to still be asleep but not quite able to sleep. I definitely needed a few more hours of shuteye; I had spent the night out with my buddies from the club lacrosse team, and I was already regretting the last pitcher of beer I bought for our table.

My phone rang, the soft ringtone too loud for my poor, aching, hungover head. I frowned when I saw it was Dylan calling me. Is he calling me from the plane? *I wondered.*

Dylan and Jules had flown down to Cabo for Callie and Ryan's destination wedding over the weekend. I was supposed to pick them up at the Eugene airport. In an hour. It only took me twenty minutes to drive there from Dylan's and my apartment, so I still had over half an hour until I had to leave.

I answered the phone hesitantly. "Dylan?" I sounded awful even to my own ears. He of all people would know I was hungover right off the bat.

"Hey, Jake. Where are you parked?"

"Um… I'm still at home. How did your plane get in so early?" I looked at my alarm clock just to be sure. Yep. Definitely only 10AM, not 11AM when I'm supposed to pick them up.

"We landed right on time, man," he said calmly, but I could tell he
~~~

wasn't too happy to hear I was nowhere near the airport.

I pulled the phone from my ear to double-check the time on my phone. Oh shit. My phone clock said 11AM. I started scrambling to get dressed, find my keys, find some shoes. "Dude I don't know what happened, but my alarm clock is an hour off," I said hastily into the phone.

Suddenly I heard Jules's voice on the other end. "Are you flipping kidding me, Jake?! Did you actually forget the time change on the day you were supposed to pick us up?!" she shouted into Dylan's phone. I pulled the phone away from my ear, wincing. The time change? Spring forward? That was today?

"I'll be there in twenty minutes," I huffed already headed for the apartment door.

In the background I heard Jules's voice again. "Tell that shithead we're getting a cab."

"Hey, man, don't worry about it. We're getting a cab," Dylan said calmly, leaving out the shithead *part.*

Before he hung up I caught only part of what Jules said next. "…why we even bothered…" I closed the door and flopped onto the couch, cursing myself for being such an idiot.

I spent the next half hour waiting for Dylan, dreading the apology I knew I would have to make. When I heard keys fumbling in the lock, I opened the door and found a very tired, slightly sunburned, but still smiling Dylan on the other side.

"I'm so sorry, man," I said sheepishly, rubbing the back of my neck nervously. "I completely forgot about the time change."

"Don't worry about it. It could happen to anyone," he said kindly, but I could see in his eyes he was disappointed in me. He carried his bags to his room then came back to the living room and headed for the door. "See ya, Jake. The cabs waiting. I'm heading over to Jules's place. Just needed to drop my bags first."

"Wait, is Jules downstairs?" I had assumed they had dropped Jules off first at her apartment just a few blocks away. Dylan nodded. "I'll go tell her I'm sorry," I said jumping up.

"I don't think that's a good idea," he warned with a shake of his head, but I ignored him and headed for the stairs. It's not like Jules being pissed at me was something new.

I found Jules in the parking lot, blond hair bleached by the Cabo sun, leaning against the cab and looking at her phone. When she saw me coming down the stairs she glanced at me then pointedly returned her eyes to her phone.

"Jules, I'm sorry I messed up the time. Even Dylan said it could happen to anyone," I said in what I hoped was an apologetic voice.

She looked up at me, her eyes narrowed like she was winding up to let me have it. "Dylan is too nice to be mad at you..." she started. Then she spotted Dylan coming down the stairs and stopped herself.

"Later, man," Dylan said slapping me on the shoulder before they climbed into the cab. As they pulled away Jules mouthed something incredibly rude at me through the window. It was so shocking, my jaw dropped. Yeah, I deserved that, *I thought ruefully as I watched them drive away.*

~~~

It stings hearing those words from Jules – that I disappoint her. I've been trying so hard to show Jules that I'm dependable, that I'm here for her and Evie. But with our history will she ever see me in that way? How can I prove it to her when I've disappointed her so many times in the past? When I've made her feel like she doesn't matter.

"If you change your mind you know where to find me," I say, as gently as I can manage, leaving Jules to deal with her own stinky mess, just like she wants me to.

Late in the evening I'm at home drinking a beer while watching a football game that I could care less about, grumbling to myself something about sports, bars, and sports bars. There's a knock at the door. I figure it's probably just a delivery, some random thing I ordered online so I ignore it. But then there's another knock. I frown, turning off the TV and setting my beer down, and head over to the door.

The blonde on my doorstep is definitely not a delivery truck driver. "Hi," Jules says, sounding somewhat shy.
~~~

I gape at her like an idiot for a few seconds. "Hey," I say, once I recover my ability to speak. I open the door wide and move aside, a silent invitation to come in. Jules stays put.

"I just came to apologize for what I said earlier. I shouldn't have said you disappoint me. You've been so great to Evie and to me, and I … I shouldn't have said that."

I lean against the door. "Jules, I know I've disappointed you plenty of times in all the years we've known each other, so it wasn't completely unexpected to hear that from you. But I hope you know you can depend on me now. I'm here to help, so just ask away and I'll try not to disappoint."

She nods, biting her lip. "I know, Jake. Thank you for saying that. It's not… it's not you I'm mad at."

"Will you just come in, Jules, or are you going to let all of the heat out of my house?" I ask, waving my arm to usher her inside.

She walks through the door offering me an apologetic smile. She stops in her tracks when she sees my kitchen.

"Oh, right. I'm remodeling," I say, rubbing the back of my neck. With the subflooring exposed, the cabinets without doors, and the gaping hole and dangling electrical wires where the fridge should be, it's a bit of a disaster. No, it's not a bit of a disaster. It's a complete disaster.

I walk over to my barely-livable kitchen and gesture to the barstools, trying to appear as though I'm not mortified.

"Are you hungry?" I ask, opening the pantry where I keep snack food.

"Always," Jules answers. I grin into the pantry at her very true self-assessment. *Someone has her appetite back,* I think, pulling some snacks out for Jules to munch on. I retrieve my beer from the living room and point to it as a silent offer. Jules shakes her head with a look of disgust. I laugh to myself, because I knew she would do that. I pour her a glass of water instead. *At least I have running water,* I think, still cursing myself for letting Jules see this disaster.

"Are you doing this yourself?" Jules asks, waving her hand at the half-finished kitchen.

"Yeah. My dad has helped out a bit, but mostly it's just been me."

"How long has it taken you?" she asks.

I take a long sip of my beer, formulating my answer. "A bit longer than I expected."

She tilts her head, eyes narrowing slightly. "Like how long is longer than expected?" she asks, not letting my vague answer slide.

I wobble my head from side to side, thinking it over. "A few months?" Once I did the major work – tearing out a wall, building the kitchen island, and installing the sink – I stalled out. I haven't had anyone over aside from my parents in so long that finishing my kitchen really hasn't been a priority for me. Keeping the fridge in the garage doesn't really bother me, and not having cabinet doors is almost more convenient. But seeing Jules's horrified look, I think maybe I should make it a priority to finish this project. The sight of my unfinished work isn't exactly supporting my claim that I'm dependable.

Jules

I shouldn't have said that Jake disappoints me. That was unfair. *Sure there have been plenty of times he has disappointed me,* I admit to myself. *Like the time he -* I stop myself. I don't need to go down that rabbit hole of old grudges. Those screwups happened years ago, and I don't want to hold onto that kind of resentment. What matters is that in the past several months, Jake has been there for Evie in so many, and he's been there for me, too. I really am lucky to have him.

But Evie can't come over here until he finishes this death trap of a kitchen.

Jake

"If you're not mad at me, what's really upsetting you?" I ask, trying to steer the subject away from my work-in-progress kitchen.

Jules raises her hands helplessly and sighs. "Everyone. Everything."

I remember that feeling all too well. "Anything specifically?" I ask with a soft chuckle.

She rakes her fingers through her hair, her mouth pressed into a hard line. "Laurel told Evie she would take her to a movie today and she bailed. I had to be the one to tell Evie, to disappoint her."

"And you asked Laurel to watch Evie." It's a statement, not a question. Jules nods. "So that you could deal with the bottle drop mess." She nods again.

I let out my breath in one loud gust of air. "That sucks." There's no way around it. That sucks.

"I have a lot of questions, but my first is, why on Earth would you ask *Laurel* for help?" I ask making a face.

Jules actually smiles at my joke. "She said something to me at Thanksgiving about wanting to spend more time with her niece, and I actually believed her. And then I thought, 'She seemed really sincere. Why not just give her a chance?' And the one time I ask her for help, she bails on me five minutes before she's supposed to show up. Without even giving me a reason!"

Self-fulfilling prophecy is the phrase that is coming to mind. Asking *Laurel* for help was the best way Jules could prove to herself that it isn't even worth asking.

"I mean this in the nicest way, Jules, but you are really bad about asking anyone for help." She frowns at me, but the way her shoulders droop at my words, I can tell she knows I'm right. "You're so good at telling people what to do," I say with a smirk that makes Jules roll her eyes. "Why is asking for help so difficult for you?"

"I don't know. But maybe I'm trying to work on it?"

"Well try harder. And don't ask Laurel. Ask me. I'd do anything for you." Jules looks up at me; our eyes lock, and I feel myself gulp reflexively. "And for Evie," I add with a shaky voice.

"OK," Jules says quietly. She munches on her snacks silently and I take an extra-long moment to finish the last of my beer. When I set the bottle down Jules is looking at me with a small grin.

"Hey, Jake. How would you like to help me with a fundraiser for Evie's school?" she asks.

I offer her a lopsided grin. "Sure, Jules. I'd love to."

CHAPTER 9

Jake

After a long round of handshaking, back slapping, and other overly masculine displays, I finally wave goodbye to JT Architects' newest clients. My dad offers me a proud smile and leads the clients down the block toward their cars. As I walk down the sidewalk in the opposite direction I finally am able to take a full breath. The pitch for the homes we will design for their new housing development went even better than expected. Work meetings like this one always require a lot of energy. I'm a pretty energetic guy, but this meeting left me feeling completely spent.

What started as a presentation at our office - a presentation that I took the lead on for the first time since joining the company – moved to dinner in a private room at a restaurant downtown and ended in a round of celebratory drinks at the bar. I'm excited to get started on the new project, but I'm glad the day-long meeting is over and I can take the rest of the evening to unwind.

As I walk I spot a familiar blonde half a block ahead of me. I would recognize those curly tresses anywhere, but something seems off about her.

"Jules! Hey wait up!" I call, jogging toward her.

She turns a bit slowly and starts doubling back to meet me. It takes me a minute to realize she's walking a bit wobblily. Like she's drunk. But that doesn't make any sense. Jules never drinks.

"Hey, Jake," she says a bit breathlessly. I notice the dainty paper bag she's carrying with the wine bottle sticking out of it. She is definitely drunk.

"What are you up to?" I ask her a bit hesitantly.

"My dad gave me the night to myself. I went to a wine bar. Special occasion," she mutters.

"What's the occasion?" I ask.

"It's my anniversary," she says with a dark smile.

My eyebrows knit together in confusion. "No, it's not. Your wedding was in the summer." I was the best man after all, I think I'd at least remember the season.

She laughs, but the sound is bitter. "Not *Dylan's* and my anniversary. *My* anniversary," she explains. I stare at her still confused and starting to become concerned. "One year a widow," she mumbles. My stomach drops as her words hit me. Dylan died a year ago. "So my dad is watching Evie and I'm... doing this," she says raising her paper bag in explanation.

"And this helps?" I ask, and I realize too late that my question comes off as scornful. Who am I to judge after the way I have reacted to loss or the way I behaved like a bourbon-soaked wrecking ball after Dylan's funeral.

Her eyes narrow at me. "Worth a shot," she snaps, turning and walking away.

I curse. "Wait, Jules, where are you going?" I ask catching up to her. "The park."

"Why the park?" I ask placing my hand on her elbow to steady her. "Seems like a great place to get drunk."

"It seems like you're already drunk," I respond teasingly.

"Fine. I'm going to the park to get *more* drunk," she huffs.

I grab her arm lightly pulling her up short. "Stop, Jules." She scowls at her elbow as though she is just now noticing my hand on her arm. I drop my hand. "Are you hungry?" I ask her.

"What?"

"Are you hungry?" I repeat.

"Why?"

"Because you're always hungry. I don't want an SAT-invalidating stomach growl situation if we're going to get drunk in the park." She punches me lightly in the arm. "You always bring that up!" she shrieks at me, and just as I intended I see something that looks almost like a smile on her face.

~~~

The classroom was silent aside from the muted sounds of pages turning and pencils scribbling on paper. There was palpable tension in the air. We were spending a Saturday taking the SAT, a test we had been told for years would basically determine our future. Partway through the math section, I heard a noise that sounded like a wildcat screaming. I looked next to me and saw Jules, her face bright red, clutching her stomach. I burst out laughing. "Was that you?" I asked her.

"It was just my stomach growling. Shut up, Jake!" she hissed at me, which made me laugh even harder.

"Mr. Thompson!" I looked up to see the exam proctor, our English teacher Mrs. Harris, standing over me, glaring at me. "Another disruption like that and I will have to invalidate your exam."

I sputtered, "But Jules is the one –"

"Enough!" Mrs. Harris cut me off and walked away.

I scowled at Jules. Her eyes had never left her exam, but her eyebrows were raised and she was pursing her lips trying to stop herself from cracking up.

Annoyed that of course I would get in trouble and not perfect Jules Nelson who had also been talking, I threw my spare pencil at her. Jules made a small indignant gasp.

"That's it, Mr. Thompson," Mrs. Harris growled. "I'm invalidating your exam. Leave the room. Now."

As I stomped out of the classroom I glared over my shoulder at Jules. I will never forget the look of absolute surprise and unabashed amusement on her face as she watched me lose about fifty bucks and an entire Saturday to my invalidated test. All because her stupid stomach growled like an
~~~

untamed beast.

~~~

"It was *your* ridiculously loud stomach that started it! My parents were so pissed. And I had to take that damn test *again* a month later."

She shoves me playfully. "That test was so long and I couldn't bring any snacks. It's not like I could help it! I was hungry! And my stomach is always growling. You just don't hear it because you are always talking!" She keeps shoving me down the sidewalk throughout her entire rant.

"Oh, *I'm* the one who's always talking," I scoff. "No. That must be why you talk so much. So no one will hear your stomach growling like a wild animal."

Jules bares her teeth at me playfully in a way that makes me absolutely howl with laughter.

"And is your stomach growling now?" I ask her.

She stops shoving me and shrugs. "Of course it is."

"Then let's feed the beast," I say grinning, putting my arm around her shoulders and leading her wobbly self to the closest place we can find take-out.

Take-out bags and wine bag in tow, we head to the park. When we arrive at the park I look around trying to figure out where Jules plans to sit. It's January in central Oregon; there's snow everywhere and it's dark. We spot a bench that is mostly free of snow and sit down. Jules pulls her wine bottle out of its dainty paper bag.

"How are you planning to open that?" I ask, wondering if she's even brought a corkscrew for her little outing.

She taps her temple and says, "I thought ahead. Screw top." She unscrews the bottle top triumphantly and takes a sip.

"You know that fancy little bag might look nice, but you're still just a hobo drinking from a paper bag in the park," I say with mock scorn.

Jules shrugs and takes another sip. She passes the bottle to me. I
~~~

take a sip, grimacing at the sweetness of the white wine, and hand it back to her. She screws the top on the bottle and slumps down in her seat.

"I'm not always like this, you know," Jules says sheepishly.

"I've known you for nearly two decades, Jules. You're never like this," I say truthfully. I've never seen Jules have more than one drink in a night. Ever.

"It's becoming my pathetic little tradition."

"Tradition? What do you mean?" I ask.

"This is how I celebrated Dylan's and my wedding anniversary, back in July. Hobo at the park, that time, too." *Did she do that all by herself?* I wonder, my heart aching for her, how alone she must have felt. How badly she had needed a friend and I wasn't there for her.

"I didn't realize you were struggling like this, Jules," I manage to say, the guilt for not being more supportive of my closest friend almost unbearable. *I should have noticed. I should have asked.*

"I'm OK, Jake," Jules assures me.

"Don't even try that 'I'm fine. I'm OK' crap on me, Jules." *I care about you too much for you to lie to me right now.*

"It's the truth. I *am* OK. Really." I give her a hard look, and she rolls her eyes at me. "Alright maybe *today* I'm not OK. All in all I'm doing fine. A lot better than I was this summer." *So she was really struggling this summer, and I was a complete crap friend who did nothing to help.*

"This day is just really hard. And I think maybe it always will be," she admits. "Just like our wedding anniversary in July will always be hard." Jules laughs suddenly. "It was a lot warmer then. What was I thinking doing this in January? This sucks."

I laugh, too. She's right. This sucks. "Let's take this party somewhere warmer. I happen to know a great spot and the owner is super chill."

"Where?" she asks.

"My place."

"Oh," Jules says quietly, her brow furrowed. *Shit. Does she think I'm making a pass at her? What kind of a twisted jerk does she think I am?*

"I don't mean… Not… That's not what I…" I sputter.

"I just don't want you to have to drive me home. It would be so out of your way," Jules explains with a guilty look on her face.

I take a breath, relieved. *So maybe she doesn't think I'm a complete monster.* "Driving you home is not an issue. You can warm up, drink a bit more of that bottle, *legally,* and I'll drive you home when you're ready."

"OK, sure," she agrees. "I haven't seen your place since you finished the remodel," she says standing up and looking a little steadier on her feet. Jules's horror at my unfinished kitchen lit a fire under me and I completed the project in just a few weeks.

"Let's go, ya' hobo," I say. Jules shakes her head at me but loops her arm through mine, and I lead her to my car.

"What do you mean you haven't been skiing this year?" I ask Jules incredulously. She is sitting on my couch, curled up under a blanket, wine *glass* (she is able to take the bottle out of the bag here) in hand. "But you love to ski. Why haven't you gone up to the mountain? You live in central Oregon now. That's what you *do* when you live here."

"I haven't gotten around to it," she says defensively. "Evie isn't quite old enough. I'm planning to take her up for her first lessons next year."

"Why don't you go by yourself?"

She stares at me like I'm an idiot. "Because I'm a single mom who works during the week and has to watch my kid on the weekends. I can't just go up to the mountain any time I want. I can't just do whatever I want whenever I want with whoever I want without any sense of consequence or responsibility."

Ouch. "I'm going to pretend that comment wasn't directed at me," I say my eyes narrowed at her. She takes a slow sip of her wine and gives me a look that makes it very clear that comment was absolutely directed at me, the *eternal* bachelor. "And if you want to go up to the mountain, I'm sure there are plenty of people who would want to watch Evie. I'll watch her any time you need me to. But you should find someone else to watch her so you can ski, because I want to go up with you," I say honestly. Jules looks surprised to hear that. "Let's go this weekend. Can't your dad watch Evie?"

Jules sighs. "I'm sure he would if I asked him, but he watches her so much when I'm working – he drops her off at preschool, he picks her up from preschool and watches her until I get home from work, he watches her so I can work out in the evenings. I just feel guilty asking him to take care of her on a weekend, too."

"I'm sure he would love to take care of his granddaughter even on a weekend, especially if it meant you could go do something fun." Jules shrugs her shoulders noncommittally.

"What about the Baileys? Laurel, no. Obviously. But what about Ellen and Michael? Wouldn't they want to watch Evie on a weekend?" I'm sure Dylan's parents would jump at an opportunity to see their granddaughter.

Jules hesitates. "I've barely heard from them since Evie and I moved here. Aside from Thanksgiving, we haven't…I thought… I hoped we would see more of them, but we've only seen them a few times." I can tell by the tone of Jules's voice that this is a really sore subject. Part of the draw of moving back to Bend was that Dylan's family would only be 30 minutes away and able to help out more. But it sounds like perhaps things with Dylan's family haven't quite panned out the way Jules expected them to.

"Maybe they're afraid to be the ones to reach out," I say gently.

"Yeah, maybe," Jules replies, unconvinced.

I slap my forehead. "Your sister! Why don't you ask Callie to watch Evie so we can ski?" From what I've seen Callie is nuts about Evie and would love a day with her niece. For the first time Jules looks like she's really thinking over the idea of skiing with me this weekend. "If you don't call her, *I will*," I say with a wicked grin.

"Oh my God, Jake, she's a married woman. Leave her alone."

"That's never stopped me before," I tease, laying back and resting my hands behind my head with a self-satisfied grin. Jules looks horrified. *Does she think I'm serious?* I sit up hastily. "I'm kidding Jules. You know I'm kidding, right?"

"No, I actually thought you were serious," she says laughing nervously.

"Why would you think that?" I sputter. *Why would she think that I would have an affair with a married woman? I'm no saint, but really?*

Jules gives me a hard look. "A mountain of evidence collected over many years."

I gape at her. "What evidence?"

"Oh, just the fact that you have hooked up with and rapidly discarded every friend I have ever had. Every. One." I open my mouth to contradict her, but I realize her assessment is fairly accurate.

"Well, they were all single," I say defensively.

"And I'm sure all of the women you were chatting up when you were downtown tonight were single, too," Jules says condescendingly.

"I was at a work meeting tonight!" I exclaim. "With my dad!"

Jules is staring at me like the idea that I would be working on a Friday night instead of out trying to pick up women just does not compute.

"All of that was a long time ago, and … and I'm not like that anymore," I add with a huff.

Jules guffaws. I scowl at her. "Since when?" she asks incredulously.

"Since … since a year ago…" I mutter, mostly to myself.

~~~

During Dylan's memorial service, I stood at the back of the church. I couldn't sit in a pew. I couldn't sit calmly in the middle of a crowd of people. I was barely holding myself together. Watching Evie and Jules walk into the service hand in hand had almost put me over the edge; I nearly walked out of the church when I saw Jules settle Evie on her lap and hold her to her chest. I only stayed because I knew, even if I was just standing at the back of the church, even if she didn't know I was there, I couldn't let Jules face that service alone.

Jules's speech about Dylan was incredible. She was funny and heartful. She told endearing stories about Dylan. She illustrated his incredible gifts as an inspiring educator, loving husband, and nurturing father. As I choked back the emotion that threatened to bubble over, I couldn't help but
~~~

wonder, not for the first time, who would give a speech about me when I died. And I wondered what they could possibly say. I knew it wouldn't be someone who loved me the way Jules loved Dylan. And I knew whatever was said would pale in comparison to what was said about Dylan. Because I wasn't half the man he was.

After that night - the night I spent too many hours at too many bars and made a regrettable visit to a liquor store - I knew that I wanted to become someone better than I was. That if the world had lost another great man, someone as extraordinary as Dylan, then I needed to do something to even out the balance of good and bad in the world. Even if I couldn't hope to be anything close to what an incredible man Dylan was, I could at least make a greater effort to stop being the bad guy.

Even though I had matured, grown, and changed in the past several years it wasn't enough. I had to keep working to become a better man. To become someone Dylan would be proud of.

~~~

Jules looks like she is about to say something.

"So are we going skiing or not?" I ask, switching gears abruptly. I know she notices the way I changed the subject, but she lets it slide.

"If Callie can watch Evie, then yes."

"Awesome! If you're hitting the mountain with me there are only three rules you have to follow." Jules rolls her eyes at me, but I ignore her. These are important rules that everyone who skis with me *must* follow. "Number 1: You have to chug a beer with me in the parking lot before we get on the first lift."

"Jake you are 29 years old! Tell me you don't still do that!"

I ignore her and continue. "Number 2: Bring your own damn chapstick. You can't borrow mine."

"That's a rule I will definitely follow," she grumbles. "And you can't borrow mine either."

"And the most important rule. Number 3: You have to wear a helmet." Jules's eyes snap to mine.

"Always," she says seriously. I nod at her, knowing that she understands better than anyone what that rule means to me.
~~~

CHAPTER 10

Jake

"Is Callie watching Evie?" I ask Jules as I drive toward the ski park.

"No, I actually called the Baileys and they were thrilled to take her for the day. You were right–"

"I'm sorry what was that?" I ask cutting her off.

She rolls her eyes. "I said, 'You were right.'" I grin at her irritation. "And after we talked for a bit we came up with a plan for how they can see her more often."

"That's great, Jules! For Evie, for them, for you. Does that mean I can convince you to hit the mountain with me a few more times this season?"

"We'll see how today goes before I make that decision," she says, sounding a bit nervous.

"When's the last time you hit the slopes?" I ask, wondering if she's just feeling a bit out of practice.

"I think two years?"

My jaw drops. "How is that possible? When we were kids you were up here almost every weekend."

Jules shakes her head. "I think you know why, if you just think about it," she says, her words slow and measured. I grimace at my own thoughtlessness. *Of course she didn't go skiing last year. She was too busy taking care of her terminally-ill husband to take a weekend to ski, you idiot.*

"Right," I say quietly.

"So don't be surprised if I'm a bit rusty," Jules says, quickly smoothing over my blunder.

I have a season pass, so I can just step out of the car and hit the slopes, but we have to go to the ticket office to buy Jules's lift ticket. While we're in line I start needling her to buy a season pass.

"Come on, Jules. You know you're going to want to come up with me more often. Dylan's parents will watch Evie. It will be so much easier if we don't have to stop here to get you a ticket every time we come. Just get the season pass," I say shaking her teasingly by the shoulders.

She pushes me away, laughing. "I'm just getting the day pass."

"Why? It just makes sense to get the season pass."

She sighs, eyes narrowed at me. I'm muttering, "Season pass, season pass, season pass," as we approach the counter.

"I'd like to get a season pass," Jules says politely to the staff member. I raise my arms in silent victory.

While we ride the ski lift to the top of the first run, I try to annoy Jules with over-the-top ski slang. "You ready to carve up the gnar? Hit the fresh pow pow."

"Please stop," Jules says, but the way her lips are pursed I can tell she's trying not to smile. I don't know why I have suddenly become the sixteen-year-old version of myself, pestering her the way I am. But I'm enjoying myself too much to stop.

Once we're off the lift, we make a cursory plan about which runs we'll take and which lift we'll meet up at. Before we take off I tap Jules's lime green helmet for luck - and because it's just plain fun to pester Jules some more.

"OK Noodle-son, let's go," I say, trying to keep a straight face.

"Ugh! No! That name is not making a comeback!" Jules shrieks.

"It's not my fault your name is Nelson and you looked like a thin piece of spaghetti when you were twelve." I didn't come up with the nickname, but I probably used it more and for much longer than anyone else. Jules punches my arm, and if it weren't for her ski gloves and my thick ski jacket I think it might actually have hurt.

"OK, OK. I'll stop. I'll meet you at the lift." I lean close and whisper, "Noodleson." I take off down the hill laughing while Jules spouts off some admonishment laced with a surprising number of profanities.

On the drive home I glance over at Jules. She has reclined her seat; she looks exhausted but the small grin that hasn't left her face all day lets me know she is very content.

"Now are you glad you bought that season pass?" I ask, trying not to look too smug.

She nods silently and when I glance back at her she has her eyes closed. I frown.

"Hey! You can't go to sleep on me. You're the co-pilot. You're supposed to entertain the driver on the ride home," I whine.

"That's what the radio's for," Jules grumbles, eyes still tightly shut.

"You haven't stopped talking for the eighteen years I've known you and you choose *now* to suddenly go quiet?"

"I'm just so warm and comfortable. These heated seats are heaven," she mumbles. "And I haven't been getting enough sleep. I can't help it."

"Why haven't you been getting enough sleep?" I ask, because I selfishly want to keep her awake. And because I actually am curious.

"Hi, Jake, nice to meet you. I'm Jules, your friend with a five-year-old daughter. *Remember*?" Jules grumbles at me.

"Is Evie not sleeping well or something? I would have thought by five years old she'd be sleeping like…I don't know… a regular person."

"Regular person," Jules echoes, chuckling, eyes still closed. "I don't know when kids sleep like regular people. But she still wakes up a few nights a week from a bad dream or some other sleep disturbance, and I have to lay with her a while until she calms down. And the worst part is the nights she doesn't wake up *I* wake up. I just sit there listening thinking 'Why am I awake? Did Evie wake me up?' and I end up going to check on her because I'm worried there's a reason I woke up. It's ridiculous and exhausting."

"I guess lack of sleep just kind of comes with the parenting territory?"

"Mhmm," Jules murmurs, snuggling into the reclined seat.

I reach over and pat her leg. "OK, I'll let you sleep, babe." My eyes widen. *What did you just call her?* I sneak a glance at Jules, but she seems to already be asleep and to not have registered what popped out of my mouth.

When I pull up to Jules's house, she is still asleep. I shake her shoulder gently. "Hey, Jules, we're here," I whisper, not wanting to startle her. She opens her eyes slowly, then looks up at me frowning.

"Did I sleep the whole way?"

"You looked like you needed it," I say honestly.

"Sorry. Some co-pilot," she grumbles.

She sits up and stretches a bit, gathering her things then reaches across the console and wraps me in a friendly hug. "Thank you for today. You're the best. I haven't had that much fun in… well, in a long time," she says in a sleepy voice. Slightly stunned, I keep one hand on the steering wheel and awkwardly pat her arm with my other hand.

After I help Jules carry her gear to her door, I drive home so lost in thought I am barely conscious of the route I take, my thoughts drifting to long, blond curls in the passenger seat of my car.

~~~

I dropped my gym bag on the floor and collapsed onto my bed. It wasn't wrestling season yet, but the pre-season workouts were already killer. As I started to change out of my sweaty clothes I saw Jules's number flash across the screen of my phone. I felt my heartbeat pick up a little, and I knew why, though I wasn't quite ready to admit it.
~~~

"Hello Miss Nelson," I answered formally.

"Hey Jake," she said ignoring my lame joke. "Can you give me a ride to the football game tonight? Long story short, I'm going home with Emma after the game and then we have a soccer tournament out of town so I don't want to leave my car at her house and —"

"I can give you a ride," I said cutting her off. 'Long story short' meant nothing to Jules. All of her stories were long. I would normally just let her talk, because I could listen to Jules talk for hours. But if I was going to give her a ride in a few minutes I would have to jump in the shower. Now.

"OK great I'll see you in a bit! And thank you, Jake. You're the best," she said hanging up.

No, I'm not, *I thought to myself.* I'm not the best. Couldn't she see that? For the past six months I had been a wrecking ball of reckless behavior - fighting, cutting class, missing curfew, drinking, getting my kicks with nearly every girl in our grade. I was the picture-perfect example of just about every teen cliché misbehavior.

And for the past few months I had been feeling this awful push and pull between wanting Jules to take an interest in me and dreading her doing so. I knew how incredible she was. She was everything I wanted, everything I would ever want.

But I knew I could never let myself get involved with her, because I would just screw it up. Like I was screwing everything up in my life, like Self-Sabotage was my middle name. And Jules deserved so much better than that. But I couldn't screw up something that never even started, so I would never let myself cross the lines of friendship with Jules. I could never let myself hurt her, so I wouldn't let myself get close enough to do that.

I wasn't doing a great job of keeping her at arm's length recently. We had been spending more time together, and giving her a ride tonight was another step too close to being something a bit more than friends.

With Jules in the front seat of my car, periodically raking her fingers through her long blond curls, telling me some long, hilarious story about something that happened in her history class, I felt myself caving to the feelings I had for her. At a red light I looked over at her and our eyes locked in a way that gave me the thrilling and terrifying notion that maybe she was feeling the same draw to me.

Jules

At the football game, Jake and I parted ways when one of my friends from my English class stopped me and Jake spotted a group of his wrestling teammates. I didn't see Jake again until a few minutes into the fourth quarter. I was heading to the concession stand and walked past two people making out. Just after I passed them I realized in a wave of embarrassment that the guy was Jake and the girl he was making out with was Emma. Emma who I was spending the night with and traveling with for the whole weekend for a soccer tournament. I kept walking, trying to ignore the jealousy, embarrassment, and disappointment I was feeling.

I had heard rumors about Jake becoming what our classmates were calling a "man-whore," working his way through making out with every girl in the junior class. Not believing or just hoping they weren't true, I had ignored those rumors. But I couldn't ignore the evidence right in front of me.

I cursed myself for feeling so upset, for caring at all. I felt like such an idiot for thinking Jake might like me. I knew he was a huge flirt, but I had somehow convinced myself it actually meant something when he flirted with me. How had I deluded myself into thinking that the Jake Thompson, the guy every girl in the junior class had at least a small crush on, might actually be interested in me? But tonight, driving me to the game then making out with the friend he knew I was spending the weekend with… he couldn't send a clearer message to me that we were just friends if he tried.

Jake

"Jules," I hissed in the middle of our math class on Monday. Her pencil stopping its scratching on the page was the only indication that she had heard me. "How was your soccer tournament?" I asked.

"We were awful. Lost every game," Jules answered flatly, eyes still on her paper.

"That sucks. I'm sorry," I said. At those words, she turned her gaze to me for the first time since class began. I was almost shocked by the complete lack of emotion when Jules's eyes met mine. Jules was nothing if not feisty, and the way she was looking at me with absolute apathy was unsettling.

"Emma told me you two are going out now," she said practically in monotone.

"Going out? Wait. What? I never said that," I sputtered.

Jules blinked slowly at me. "Good luck figuring that out." She turned back to her work, ignoring me completely.

I realized with a sinking feeling that there was no danger of Jules being interested in me anymore. That's a good thing. That's what you wanted, I tried to reassure myself. We could just be friends, like we should be. And that was what I wanted. Wasn't it?

~~~

On my drive home, it hits me that feelings I've buried deep down for so many years, under layer upon layer of denial and guilt, are starting to find their way to the surface. And this time, I don't know if I want to stop them.
~~~

CHAPTER 11

Jake

I'm just packing up to head home at the end of the work week when my phone rings. I feel a small thrill when I see that it's Jules calling me.

"Hey, Jules."

"Hey, Jake, do you have plans tonight?" she asks, almost sounding nervous.

My heartrate picks up for reasons I can't quite ignore. "Not yet. What's up?"

"I might need a favor."

"Oh," I say, trying not to sound disappointed. *Disappointed over what?* But then I realize that, for once, she's actually asking for my help. That's a huge step for her. "Sure, how can I help?"

"Do you remember that one time you told me you could watch Evie for me if I needed?"

"Yes, I remember," I say slowly, enjoying teasing her a bit, making her have to actually ask for my help, which I know, even if she's trying, she still hates to do.

"I hate to ask," she says hesitantly. *I know you do*, I chuckle to myself. "It's just my dad isn't feeling well and Sarah invited me to dinner tonight. I've kind of been looking forward to it and I don't want to cancel. If you can't that's fine, I totally understand. I know it's a Friday so you might have a date or something –"

"Sure, Jules," I say cutting her off. "I can watch Evie. I'll head over to your place now."

"Thank you, Jake! You're the best!" I can't ignore the way those words affect me, making my heart swell with pride.

"So when are kids old enough to watch *Terminator*?" I deadpan. Jules is silent on the other end. "I'm kidding, Jules! I'll see you in a bit."

Evie greets me at the door. "That can't be Evelyn!" I say in mock surprise. "No, you are far too grown up to be Evelyn. Where is Evie?" I ask, looking behind her.

She giggles. "It's me, Uncle Jake!"

I scoop her up in a hug. After I release her she dashes off to the living room and I follow her. We play with some magnetic building tiles that are completely fascinating. "Do you like building things, Evie?" I ask her.

"I'm good at building things," she says, eyes never leaving her creation.

"You know, I really like building, too. I design buildings," I tell her.

"You do?" she asks, looking at me with surprise. "Wow! Can I see your building?"

"Sure, sweet pea. I'll take you on a tour of some of my buildings sometime," I say proudly.

Soon Evie is regaling me with an unending story about someone getting in trouble for stepping on a book in her preschool class, and I am chuckling to myself realizing she has her mother's gift for longwinded stories. Jules walks into the living room wearing a simple, black, long sleeved dress, her long blond ringlets pulled back into a low, artfully twisted ponytail. It takes me a few awkward seconds to find my voice, but I finally clear my throat and manage to say, "You look nice."

She smiles at me. "Thanks," she says quietly, a hint of color reaching her cheeks. She holds up a piece of paper. "I wrote down Evie's schedule and a few other notes in case you have any questions. My dad is just going to be in his room, but he's here if there's an emergency."

"Bedtime's midnight, right?" I ask.

Jules purses her lips, but I can tell she's trying not to laugh. "Stop it. Bedtime is 8:00. It's on the schedule."

"Mommy has a date," Evie says, eyes back on her building tiles. "What?" I ask, confused. *Did she just say a* date? Jules's face has gone completely pink. She motions for me to join her in the kitchen.

Once we're out of Evie's earshot I ask, "You have a date?" I'm trying to keep my voice down, but I hear a distinctive edge to my voice. Jules busies herself with putting things in her purse. "I thought you were having dinner with Sarah." *Sarah, your friend from high school, college, and now work. Your friend who is definitely a married woman and not a date.*

"I am," she answers defensively. "But Brad is coming, too, and he's bringing a friend that he wants me to meet." I know and like Sarah's husband, Brad, but as of this moment I can't stand the jerk.

"And you told Evie, your five-year-old, you're going on a date? Do you think that was appropriate?" I ask, hearing the reproach in my voice.

Jules's eyes narrow, the way they always do when she's about to lecture me. I brace myself, already regretting my words. "For one, *I'm* not the one who said that. My dad did in front of her without thinking," she hisses at me. "And another it is not up to *you* to decide what is or isn't appropriate for *my* daughter."

Jules brushes past me, going back to the living room and kneeling to give Evie a kiss and hug.

"You have fun with Uncle Jake, sweet pea, and I'll come kiss you goodnight when I'm home," Jules says tenderly.

"Mommy did you know Uncle Jake makes buildings?" Evie asks.

"Yes, I did know that, sweet pea. He's pretty amazing isn't he," Jules says, giving Evie another kiss on the top of her head then heading for the door.

Why am I mad at her? I should be happy for her that she's started dating, that she's ready for that. Shouldn't I?

Jules doesn't even glance my way as she passes me. I follow her to the door, catching her arm to stop her before she leaves. She keeps her eyes down, refusing to look at me. "Jules, wait. You're right. That wasn't my place. I'm sorry. I shouldn't have said that," I say in a low voice.

When she finally looks up at me, I notice the tension in her eyes. She almost looks afraid and I feel an overpowering need to comfort her.

She lets out a long sigh. "I'm sorry I snapped like that. I'm just nervous I guess."

I squeeze her hand. "Have a great time tonight. I mean it."

She offers me a tight smile. "Thanks. You too," she says finally giving me a real grin and inclining her head to the living room where *my* date for the evening is waiting for me.

After the door closes behind her I linger in the entryway letting out a sigh. *But don't have too much fun,* I moan to myself.

~~~

In late September of our freshman year, we were at a U of O home football game. It had started out a warm afternoon, but as always happens in the Pacific Northwest, once the sun started to go down the temperature began to drop.

I had come prepared with a sweatshirt. When I saw Jules starting to shiver a bit I was almost tempted to offer her my sweatshirt, but decided against it. I brought the sweatshirt to wear it myself after all. A few minutes later I looked over to see Dylan wrapping Jules in his own zip-up hoodie. The hoodie was comically large on Jules.

I trained my eyes on the field, but I couldn't stop myself from glancing at the two of them out of the corner of my eye as she thanked him for the sweatshirt. Jules looked up at Dylan like he'd hung the moon and stars, and he smiled back at her completely returning her adoration. I wanted to close my eyes but I couldn't stop myself from watching her wrap her arms around his neck, stretch up on her toes, and kiss him.
~~~

For two years I had almost convinced myself that I wasn't completely in love with Jules. That we were friends and only friends. But seeing her kiss Dylan I knew that I had been fooling myself. It's better this way, I reminded myself. Dylan is a great guy. Much better for Jules than you could ever be. It's better this way.

Trying to cover my own heartbreak, I wolf-whistled at the two of them. They broke apart, startled, and turned to me laughing nervously. I grinned at them in a way that I thought was believable. I slapped Dylan on the back, saying, "Atta boy. I knew you had it in you."

Later that night I made out with Megan, Jules's roommate. Even though Jules told me to stay away from her. **Because** *Jules told me to stay away from her. I knew I would never be the good guy, so I might as well embrace the role.*

~~~

"So, Miss Evelyn," I say as I walk into the living room. She looks up at me with her big blue eyes. "What are your feelings about mac and cheese?" Her eyes light up and she starts bouncing in place, grinning from ear to ear.

Jules

I walk into the living room to find Jake folding a blanket. When he spots me, his eyes widen and he gapes at me like he's horrified to see me. "What are you doing home so soon?"

I look at the clock on the wall. "It's 10:00, Jake. I haven't been out this late since Evie was born."

"Well I … I… I didn't expect you home so soon," he sputters. "I…I didn't finish cleaning up yet. I'm sorry."

I look behind him to see a giant blanket fort that he and Evie must have made. There are drawings scattered all over the floor – some of Evie's creations and several of Jake's sketches. I imagine I will find several of his drawings in her room later tonight, taped to her wall. Jake looks embarrassed as though he believes the living room is a disastrous mess.

I shrug. "Looks like a normal Friday night." I grab one of the
~~~

blankets from the fort, kick off my shoes, and stretch out on a couch wrapped up in the blanket. "You should have seen this place when my dad had to watch Evie when I had parent-teacher conferences. I got home at 9PM, Evie was still up, and I think every toy that she owns was in this room." Jake folds a few more blankets and picks up the majority of the drawings then settles on the other couch.

"It looks like you had fun," I say gesturing to the remnants of the blanket fort.

"We did. We really did," he says with a huge smile. "Your kid is awesome, Jules. And I have to admit we didn't quite make the 8:00 bedtime. It was probably closer to 9:00," he says apologetically, rubbing the back of his neck in his nervous way.

I shrug. "Close enough."

"So how was dinner?" he asks somewhat hesitantly.

"Exhausting," I admit.

"Why?" Jake asks, confused. I know he has dated a lot, *a lot* of women, so going on a date for him must be like driving to work. He could do it half asleep and get to the end of it wondering how he got there.

I sigh. "Because I haven't been on a first date since I was 18 and then going on a date was just 'Meet me for dinner at the dining hall' or 'Let's watch TV and make out in my dorm room while my roommate's gone.'" Jake makes the same gagging noise he always did whenever he would interrupt romantic moments between Dylan and me, which tonight makes me laugh.

"And even though this guy tonight – Crap what was his name? John? Yeah, John. Or was it Jim?" Jake is cracking up because I don't even remember my date's name, but I ignore him. "Anyways, even though *this guy* whatever his name was tonight seemed nice enough, I knew that within the first five minutes he was ready to run."

"Why would you think that?" Jake asks, taken aback.

"Because it's true! 'Hi Jules, nice to meet you. I'm Jim or John or whatever the hell my name is. I hear you're a teacher. You must like children, then. Oh, you have one? Wait she's how old? Wait how old are you then? Oh. And you're a widow? You don't say. At the age of 29? Wow. That's a lot to take in. And whoa you talk a lot. Oh and you live with your… dad… Check please.' It's just a lot. Too much. And I'm just… too much." I cover my eyes with my hand and shake my head. When I open my eyes I'm startled to see Jake's dark eyes so close to mine; he has suddenly appeared, sitting on the floor next to me.

"Oh, hi," I say awkwardly, surprised by his sudden proximity.

"Jules, you are not too much. Never think that," he says earnestly. "So this John or Jim or Jefferson, whatever his name was, just think of that dinner as a drill or a scrimmage before an actual game."

Sports, bars, and sports bars, I think, chuckling to myself about his sports reference. "Ugh that almost makes it sound worse. I'll have to go on so many dates if I ever want to find someone who will take all of *this* on, forever," I whine as I gesture to myself and the remnants of the blanket fort.

"Is that what you want?" he asks.

"Well, I guess I'm not so naïve anymore to think anyone can promise *forever*." No one can promise that. "But yeah," I say, shrugging. "I'm only 29. I want a partner. I want Evie to grow up with a dad. I want more children. I don't want to live the rest of my life like mine ended when Dylan's did," I huff.

I can tell something I said surprises Jake by the way his eyes widen during my rant. But I just said a lot of things, like I always do, so I don't know what it was.

"Do you feel ready for that? Ready to… move on, I guess, for lack of a better term?" he asks.

"I don't think I'll ever really be ready, but I know I need to move forward even if I'll probably never really move on."

Jake's mouth presses into a firm line, like he's thinking something over. "Then if you need someone to watch Evie another time for another date, though I doubt it will be with John or Jim or Jefferson or Jebediah whatever the hell his name was, I would be happy to watch her any time."

"So you're not mad at me?" I ask, internally rolling my eyes at myself for how timid my voice sounds to my own ears. *Why do I care so much if Jake's mad at me?*

"Mad at you? Why would you think that?" Jake asks, frowning.

"You seemed so upset with me earlier. I thought maybe you felt I was … I don't know… being disloyal to Dylan or something." *Or maybe that was just me, projecting my own feelings.*

"I don't think that," he says, his frown deepening. "That's not something you need to worry about. OK?" I offer a small nod, and he rubs the back of his neck in his nervous way, choosing his words. "I know how much you loved Dylan, how much he loved you. Trying to move forward with your life doesn't change that." He sighs. "I was just surprised tonight and I shouldn't have been. You're a gorgeous girl, and…"

I smile coyly at him. He's never given me such an unmistakable compliment. He shakes his head, smiling at me.

"Don't look at me like that. You know it's true." I wave my hand at him as if to say *Continue.* "And I shouldn't be surprised that other guys are going to take an interest."

Jake stops talking suddenly, frowning again. I can't tell if he's lost his train of thought or just doesn't know what else to say.

I reach over, tousling his hair and say, "You're a good guy. Thank you."

"I should hit the road," Jake says standing up. He offers me his two hands to help me up from the couch. I take his hands, and he lifts me from the couch in one quick, playful tug that makes me yelp in surprise and sets me giggling.

He grins at me mischievously, like he needed to be a bit rascally to counteract my *good guy* praise. "Thanks for letting me spend some time with my goddaughter." He stares at me for a moment as though he's being indecisive about something then heads to the door.

I follow him to the door and lock up behind him then trudge up the stairs. I peak into Evie's room and see that she is sleeping with her feet facing the headboard without even a blanket on top of her. *How does she sleep like that?* Like I told her I would, I sneak in and give her a kiss.

A few minutes later I'm lying in bed, wrapped in Dylan's

bathrobe as is my habit on particularly cold or trying nights. I'm desperate to fall asleep knowing Evie will be up around 5:30. But because I'm a parent, and to parents a good night's sleep is more valuable than gold and more elusive than Sasquatch, it takes me hours to fall asleep.

CHAPTER 12

Jules

"I have something for you. In my lunch bag," Jake says, motioning toward the bag stuffed behind his car's center console as we drive home from another great day of skiing on the mountain. I unzip the bag and find a giant Reese's Easter egg.

"I love these!" I gasp. "Thank you!" I gush, clutching the giant candy to my chest.

He grins proudly. "I saw it at the store and knew you liked them." I stare at him, grinning like a fool. "What?" he asks when he glances over at me still staring at him. I can't believe he remembered how much I like this candy and that he would think to buy it for me. He can be so sweet when he wants to be.

"You just surprise me sometimes," I say, tearing into the Easter egg and breaking off a piece that I place in his outstretched hand.

"I surprise you?" he asks incredulously around a mouthful of chocolate and peanut butter. "You're the surprising one," he mutters as an afterthought.

"How am *I* surprising?" I ask, baffled.

Jake chews slowly, like he's deciding what to say. "You said something recently that surprised me."

"What did I say?"

"You said you wanted to have more children," he answers. "That surprised me."

"What?" I ask, taken aback. That was not *at all* what I was expecting to hear.

"You said that. The other night. You said you wanted to have more children."

I remember his look of surprise during my long tirade, and it dawns on me that's what I said that surprised him.

"Well, yeah, Evie's incredible. Why wouldn't I want more?" I say with a shrug, between bites of my precious Easter egg, that I know will be gone by the time we are home.

"I thought you and Dylan were one and done since you didn't have any more kids after Evie."

"Dylan told you Evie was a surprise," I say offhandedly. We didn't exactly advertise that our baby had been a surprise, but I'm sure Dylan shared that with his best friend of all people.

"Uh… no," Jake says with a stunned look. "He did not tell me that."

Oh.

~~~

Dylan and I were still on summer vacation in the months between when we finished our master's program and when we would start work. We had only been married about five weeks.

I was waiting for Dylan to come home from playing pick-up basketball; he was always in a good mood after playing basketball. And I needed him to be in a good mood if I was going to tell him what I had to tell him.

He came into the kitchen, where I was sitting at the table, and gave me a quick kiss. "Hey, babe, I'm just going to take a quick shower. Do you have something planned for dinner or do you want me to cook something?"

I bit my lip, unsure how to say what I needed to tell him.

"You're quiet," he said sitting down in the chair next to me, sensing my unease. Quiet was definitely not typical from me. "Is everything OK?"

"Yeah," I said my voice unnaturally high. "Um, do you remember our
~~~

flight back from our honeymoon, how we got in late on a Saturday?"

"Sure," he said, forehead wrinkled in confusion.

"Well the next day was Sunday, and the pharmacy was closed."

"OK," he said, still confused.

"So, um, I wasn't able to get my prescription filled until Monday."

"OK," he repeated.

"My birth control prescription."

"OK," he said, still not understanding. I saw his expression change the moment he realized what I was saying. His eyes went wide then darted to my stomach, then my face, then my stomach again. "Oh!" he repeated.

"So, um, surprise? I guess I'm making you a first anniversary gift that will arrive a couple months early?" I said in a quiet voice. I searched his face, trying to get a sense of his feelings about our momentous, unexpected news.

He raked his fingers through his thick, dark hair and let out a loud breath. "OK... that's... amazing!" he exclaimed, pulling me from the chair and wrapping me in a tight hug. When he released me he saw the tears running down my face. "Hey, Jules, this is amazing. It really is," he said softly, running his thumbs across my cheeks to gently wipe away my tears.

Aside from Callie and my dad, Dylan was the only person who had seen me cry. Plenty of times, too. He was the only person I had ever trusted enough to be that vulnerable, trusted to hold me up in the most difficult or overwhelming times.

"I know it's amazing," I blubbered. "It's just scary, and not exactly when we planned, and I can't believe I haven't even started my new job and I'll have to tell them I'm going to need time off eight months from now, and we don't even have our new health insurance until next month, and..."

Dylan stopped my blubbering monologue with a kiss. My whole body relaxed as I sank into his embrace.

Once I had quieted, he pulled back, holding my face gently in his hands. "It is scary and not happening when we planned, but we're going to have a baby!"

"Yeah, we're going to have a baby," I echoed, smiling weakly.

"I love you," Dylan said, grinning from ear to ear. He leaned down, *speaking to the tiny, delightful surprise growing inside me, saying, "And I love you." He looked up at me, eyes sparkling. "Who should we tell first?!" he asked with unbridled excitement.*

Jake

I held the phone to my ear, completely speechless. I closed my eyes and gathered the courage to say what I knew I should say. "That's amazing, man! Wow, Dylan! Congratulations! I'm so happy for you two." And then with complete honesty I said, "You're going to be an incredible dad. You lucky bastard."

After I hung up I opened my cabinet and pulled out every liquor bottle I had and spent the evening sampling each one, getting the-girl-I'm-crazy-about-is-having-my-best-friend's-baby drunk.

The next morning I did the only thing I could do. I buried my feelings for Jules under a pile of guilt and regret the size of Mt. Bachelor, so deep those feelings would never see the light of day again. Or so I thought.

~~~

Jules

"I always just assumed you wanted kids right away and that's why you had Evie so soon after you got married," Jake says, still looking astonished by my admission.

I offer a shaky, embarrassed laugh. "No, definitely not. I did not want kids right away and neither did Dylan. We were only 23 when we got married. We figured we were young enough we could just enjoy most of our twenties without kids. We planned to wait until, well, *now* to have kids. It was a huge shock to find out five weeks after our wedding day that we were pregnant.

"But I realized later it all worked out the way it should have. If we had waited Dylan never would have been a father. And I never would have been a mom. We were planning to have another eventually, but..." I lift my hands helplessly, because Jake and I both know the end of that sentence. "And with how wonderfully things went with Jehoshaphat the other night I know I'm really, really lucky to have Evie." The names we have come up with for
~~~

my unfortunately forgettable date from the other night just keep getting better.

Jake frowns. "I'm not disagreeing with you that you are incredibly lucky to have Evie, but what does that have to do with Jeronimo?" Jake asks.

I shake my head. He is being so dense. "I can't believe your parents never talked to you about this," I say trying to keep a straight face, "but when a man and woman love each other very much –"

"Stop," he says covering my mouth with his hand while I cackle with laughter. "I think I have a handle on how babies are made," he growls, placing his hand back on the steering wheel and straightening his broad shoulders. "Seriously, though, what does one crappy date have to do with you being lucky to have Evie?"

"Because my crappy date with Jericho just further opened my eyes to my slim odds of finding someone. I am so lucky to have Evie because if I hadn't already been married and had her, I would probably never have the chance to be a mom."

Jake shakes his head at me. "I do not think that's true. But you know you had it pretty easy the first time around. For most people it's not as easy as meeting your hot friend's roommate then instantly falling in love with that hot friend's roommate."

"Oh my God, stop calling yourself *hot friend*," I say rolling my eyes at him.

"I'm sure that's how you talk about me. *My hot friend Jake*," he says with a sly grin.

"No. I usually say *that scoundrel Jake*," I shoot back.

"What? Scoundrel?" Jake says clutching his chest dramatically as if my very true words wound him.

"And the context was usually, 'You don't want to get involved with that scoundrel Jake.' But they never listened. Nope. Soon after I would have to hear, 'Why did I ever get involved with that scoundrel Jake?' and I would just shake my head and try not to say 'I told you so.'"

Jake's mouth hangs open. "Wow *that scoundrel Jake* sounds like a jerk. Good thing I'm just your *hot friend* Jake," he says rubbing the back of his neck sheepishly.

I can't help but laugh at the scoundrel.

"So maybe I did have involvement with a *few* of your friends," he admits.

"A few?" I scoff.

"Yes *a few*," he reiterates.

"Let's see," I say starting to tick off names on my fingers. "There was Emma, Marissa, Audrey, Nicole, Megan... Who else?" I wonder aloud, drumming my fingers on chin just for show. "Oh yes, Steph, Leah, Rachel, Erin, Janie-"

"Alright I get the point," Jake huffs, cutting me off.

"Janie's the last one I can remember anyway," I say, kind of enjoying the fact that he at least seems a little embarrassed that I'm finally calling him out on this. "And I think the only reason you aren't seeing anyone right now is that you've been with every one of my friends and now there isn't anyone left," I say with a note of admonishment that I can't keep out of my voice.

Jake gives me a sidelong glance. "Yeah maybe something like that," he mutters.

Jake

We're less than a half hour from home when Jules's phone rings. "It's just my dad. I bet he wants me to pick up dinner. Hi, Dad," Jules answers. I see her face fall and I know something is wrong. I listen helplessly to the half-conversation. "We're on our way now; we should be there in twenty minutes... OK...That's what I would have done, too... OK... We'll be there soon. Thank you, Dad. I love you."

"Is everything OK?" I ask trying not to sound too alarmed.

Jules rakes her fingers through her hair. "Something happened in Redmond that really upset Evie. My dad had to drive over there to pick her up she was so upset. He just got her home but she is still upset and she won't tell him why."

"I'll get you home as soon as I can," I say patting her leg in what I hope comes across as a supportive gesture. "I wonder what happened."

She gives me a funny look. "Here's the really interesting part," Jules says with a half-smile. "She keeps asking for you."

I watch from the hallway as Jules steps into Evie's room. She is sitting on her bed, hugging a stuffed bunny and flipping through picture books. Her eyes are red and she is scrubbing at her cheek.

"Evie, sweetie?" Jules says softly as she sits on the edge of Evie's bed and starts rubbing her back and stroking her hair. "Bobpa said you were having a hard day. Do you want to tell me what happened?"

"I want Uncle Jake," she says softly. Jules catches my eye and nods at me to enter the room.

"Hey, sweet pea," I say kneeling on the floor next to her bed. "I heard something upset you. Do you want to tell me what's going on?"

"Uncle Jake, you're not really my uncle," she blubbers, fresh tears in her eyes.

What? Jules catches my eye and shrugs at me over the top of Evie's head, clearly just as confused as I am.

"What makes you say that, sweet pea?" I ask gently.

Evie takes a shuddering breath. "Auntie Laurel says I'm going to have a new uncle, Uncle Ian. And I was excited. I say I'll have three uncles now," she says holding up three fingers proudly. Then she frowns again, "But Auntie Laurel says no I only have two uncles. Uncle Ryan and Uncle Ian. Auntie Laurel says Uncle Jake is not my uncle. And I say yes he is and she says no and she yelled at me." Evie starts sobbing. I sit on the bed and pull her onto my lap. She sobs into my shoulder. Jules and I have a silent discussion over the top of Evie's head.

'I don't know what to do,' Jules mouths, looking uncharacteristically bewildered, her dark eyes wide with worry.

I shrug feeling just as bewildered and also like I want to drive to Redmond just to tell Laurel off for upsetting my goddaughter like this. I'm sure Laurel hates that her niece calls *me,* that idiot Jake, 'Uncle.'

"Well, sweet pea, you are going to have a new uncle, Uncle Ian, because your Auntie Laurel is going to marry Ian and that makes him your uncle. And that's really special that you're going to have a new uncle," I say, trying to control my anger at Laurel and be as positive as possible for Evie's sake. "And you are going to be the prettiest flower girl ever." Evie offers a small giggle. "And you already have an Uncle Ryan," I continue, "because he married your Aunt Callie. And both your Uncle Ian and your Uncle Ryan love you a lot."

Evie looks up at me with big, sad eyes. "But you're not my uncle?"

"Well technically, I'm not," I say tentatively, and Evie's face falls. I hurriedly continue. "When you were born, your mommy and daddy asked me to be your godfather."

Evie's forehead wrinkles. "What's that?"

"A godfather is someone who promises to always love you and take care of you. And I do love you and I will always take care of you, sweet pea. Your mommy and daddy just started calling me *Uncle* Jake because *Godfather* Jake sounds so silly," I say tickling her. Evie giggles softly, though her forehead is still wrinkled in deep thought.

"But you can call me anything you like, Evie. It doesn't matter what you call me, I'll still love you just the same if you call me Uncle Jake or just Jake or Hey You Stinky Guy. So if you don't want to call me Uncle Jake anymore that's OK with me."

Evie thinks over my explanation but she still seems very upset. Jules strokes her hair. "Is there something else bothering you sweetheart?" Jules asks. Evie nods. *Mom sixth sense*, I think to myself.

"Mindy says it's bad I don't have a daddy," she mumbles. I feel myself tense. I haven't heard Evie talk about her dad since he passed.

"Mindy from your class?" Jules asks, taking deep breaths in a way that makes me think she's heard this Mindy's name a few times before. Evie nods.

"Well, sweetie that's silly that Mindy would say that because everyone knows you *do* have a daddy," Jules says. She stands and walks over to Evie's dresser. She returns with a framed photograph. It's a picture taken on Evie's fourth birthday of Evie, Jules, and Dylan. "You know that's your daddy," Jules says pointing to Dylan in the photo. Dylan when he was still with us, when there was still hope that he might beat his illness.

Evie nods. "I know that's Daddy. At my birthday party," she says thoughtfully.

"That's right," Jules says smiling. "You know your daddy was really sick so he can't be here with us anymore, but you do have a daddy. When Mindy says you don't have a daddy you can tell her you do have a daddy. And he's in heaven."

"OK," Evie says sounding not at all convinced. An idea comes to mind.

"You know, Evie, your daddy was my best friend. I know a lot about him. And I know lots of stories about him that I can tell you."

Evie looks at me wide-eyed. "Tell me," she says with a small smile.

Jules gives me a look. *'PG stories only,'* she mouths, making me grin. I spend the next twenty minutes regaling Evie with some of my best stories about Dylan. I try to tone them down or skip over some of the more grown-up parts. Somehow nearly every story involves *root beer*. I'll tell her the PG-13 versions when she's older. I draw a quick cartoon of a memorable *root beer* drinking moment when I tried to carry Dylan piggyback style down a flight of steps and we ended up a banged-up heap of skinned limbs laughing hysterically at the bottom of the steps. Evie thinks my drawing is so funny she insists, to Jules's dismay, to tape the cartoon to her wall.

After lots of laughter and many more hugs and cuddles, Evie seems to be feeling a lot better.

"I think it's your dinner time, sweet pea," I say, lifting her off of my lap and setting her on the floor. My legs fell asleep at least half an hour ago.

"I bet your grandpa made a pot roast," Jules says winking at me, a private joke that goes way back. We all walk downstairs. I get one last hug from Evie before she skips into the living room to tackle

Robert in a big hug. I head to the door and Jules follows me. She closes the door behind her.

"Thank you, Jake. I don't know how I would have handled that without you. Thank you for… for everything," she says her voice cracking. And then the unexpected happens - Jules starts crying. I've never seen her cry. In all the years I've known her. In the months of Dylan's illness, after he passed, in everything she's been through, I've never seen her cry. Until now.

In an instant I'm holding her as she sobs into my chest. I act instinctively, trying to comfort her. I rub her back, kiss the top of her head, and murmur nonsense to her, "Shh…it's OK…shh…I've got you."

Jules relaxes her hold on me and catches her breath. I'm still holding her as she says in a voice raw with pain, "I keep thinking it will get easier, but it just gets harder."

"I want to say 'I know' but I really don't know, Jules," I say honestly. "But I do know that you are incredible. And I am always here for you, Jules. Through anything, I'm here for you."

I feel Jules still at my words. She nods her head and tightens her hold on me.

"And," I continue, "I am always on standby to tell the PG version of all of Dylan's and my best *root beer* drinking stories." Jules offers a watery laugh, then pulls away from me wiping her tears with her sleeve.

"Your shirt is all wet," she says, touching the spot on my chest that is damp with her tears. "Sorry," she mumbles.

I look down at her hand on my shirt. "I kind of like seeing physical evidence that you actually do have tear ducts," I say with a small smirk, wiping a remaining tear from her cheek.
"Yeah yeah yeah," she responds as she rolls her eyes with a small smile and shoves me lightly. I step off the porch still smirking at her and head to my car. She calls to me as I walk down the path, "And try to think of some stories about you and Dylan than don't involve *root beer!*"

CHAPTER 13

Jules

After another incredible day of skiing, Jake pulls up to my house and I notice my dad's old Forester sitting in the driveway. "My dad must already be back with Evie. Why don't you come in to see her?"

"I'd love to see my girl, but are you sure that's OK?" he asks hesitantly.

"Um… of course it's OK. I'm inviting you," I say slowly, confused by his question.

He rubs the back of his neck nervously. "I mean are you sure it's OK with your dad?"

I laugh. "What's that supposed to mean?"

"It's just that…" Jake trails off, looking conflicted. "I just don't want to show up unannounced. The last time I did that your dad didn't seem too thrilled."

"Oh," I reply, surprised. I hadn't even noticed, but I know my dad can be pretty intimidating. With his gruff voice and burly build, he scared the daylights out of most of the boys Callie and I knew growing up. I consider Jake's hesitation. Maybe it would be better if I didn't surprise my dad with an uninvited guest. And maybe he isn't overly fond of Jake for whatever reason. I drum my fingers on the dashboard while I think.

"I have an idea," I say, pulling out my phone. "Back the car up."

"What?" Jake asks completely bewildered by my instructions.

I type in the number and press send. "Just do it. Back up. Down the block. I'm sure they haven't seen us."

"Again. What?" he asks still confused.

"Shh!" I hiss and point at my phone. The call connects. "Hi, Dad! I'm just a few minutes away and Jake was wondering if you and Evie wanted us to pick up takeout for dinner."

He doesn't respond right away, probably trying to decide if this is a question he can actually say 'no' to. "That'd be great, honey. Any chance you're close to that buffet I like?" my dad asks.

"We sure are. Do you want sweet and sour soup?"

"Yes, please. And don't forget the fortune cookies," my dad reminds me, making me smile. He has an unbelievable sweet tooth.

"OK, Dad. We'll be there in about half an hour." I hang up and smile sweetly at Jake. "Problem solved. Advance notice *and* you're buying him his favorite dinner."

"Oh, so I'm buying now?" Jake scoffs.

I shrug. "Yep."

Jake

Robert is in a much better mood than he was the morning he stumbled upon me in his living room. Jules was right: advance notice and buying his favorite meal seemed to help. Over dinner he and I talk some about my latest work projects and of course Pac-12 sports. He's a die hard UCLA Bruin but he roots for the Ducks as long as they're not playing the Bruins. Even in a better mood, Robert Nelson still scares the shit out of me.

"I'm going to put this one to bed," Jules says about an hour after dinner, tousling Evie's hair. "Time to say good night, sweet pea," she says gently kissing Evie on the top of her head.

Evie collects the pile of drawings that we have been working on, saying, "I want to hang these in my room." I notice Jules's tight smile and I chuckle to myself thinking there isn't an inch of visible wall in Evie's room. Evie walks over to her grandpa and hugs him.

"Good night, Bobpa," she says in her sweet, high voice.

"Good night, sweet girl," Robert says softly, his gruff voice almost tender.

Evie walks over to me and gives me a hug, too, and to my absolute delight gives me a sweet, tiny, heart-melting kiss on the cheek. Jules scoops up Evie and carries her up the stairs. Evie's long limbs dangle as Jules croons, "My sweet, little, five-year-old baby, aw, she's so tiny." Evie shrieks with laughter all the way up the stairs. Robert and I watch them climb the stairs and disappear around the corner. I'm still smiling when I turn around, but my face falls when I take in Robert staring at me, his eyes slightly narrowed in a way that reminds me of Jules when she's winding up for one of her lectures.

He points to the stairs. "Those girls are my world."

"I know that, sir." *Sir? Where did that come from? Why do I feel like I'm sixteen?*

"They have been through a lot. Too much. And they deserve the best," he says, practically growling.

I swallow, involuntarily. "Absolutely," I say nodding my agreement. They do deserve the best. Jules has always deserved the best.

~~~

At the end of our fourth year at U of O, Dylan, Jules and the majority of our friends were graduating. I still had to complete my fifth year in the architecture program, so I attended their graduation ceremony as a spectator. It felt a little surreal watching nearly all of my friends graduate without sitting beside them. Even though I knew I was on track, that architecture is just by nature a five-year program, it still felt like I was somehow falling behind.

After the ceremony, I walked over to the spot where our group of friends had planned to meet to take pictures before heading to the party Dylan and I were throwing at our apartment. I was already feeling a bit down after the ceremony, thinking about all of the changes that were happening.

As I approached the meeting place I noticed a small commotion. All of
~~~

our friends and their families were circling around Dylan and Jules, their cameras clicking away madly. To my shock I saw that Dylan was on one knee, his hands extended to Jules, offering something in a small, open box. Jules's look of absolute joy told me everything I needed to know. When she extended her hand for Dylan to slip the ring on her finger, I looked away, unable to witness the moment she said yes.

This is what you wanted, *I reminded myself.* You wanted her to be with the someone who deserved her, and no one deserves her more than Dylan. This is what you wanted.

When I heard the applause and cheers from our friends and families and the bystanders who had stopped to enjoy the blissful moment, I took a steeling breath, ignored the ache in my chest, and put on a giant smile that I hoped was believable. I watched as Jules's dad hugged her, tears streaming down the big man's face. He shook Dylan's hand then pulled him into a tight hug, saying something in his ear that made Dylan's smile broaden.

I found my way to Dylan and wrapped him in a tight bear hug. "You sly dog. You never even told me," I said, trying my best to appear as excited as I should be.

Dylan beamed back at me. "I knew you couldn't keep a secret."

I can keep at least one secret, *I thought to myself darkly. I shrugged and said, "That's true. Good call."*

When Jules held her arms out to me, I wrapped her in a light hug. I should have just released her and smiled but I couldn't help myself. I whispered in her ear, "I'm happy for you, Jules. He's the only guy who could ever deserve you." When we broke apart Jules opened her mouth to say something, but someone else was suddenly hugging and congratulating her and I was able to slip away before I opened my stupid, heartbroken mouth again.

~~~

Robert gives me a long, scrutinizing look.

"I'm not too sure about you, Jacob. My girls talk all the time. And they seem to think I'm not listening. But the thing is, I'm always listening. I used to overhear a lot of stories about you back
~~~

when Callie and Jules were younger. And those stories didn't make me overly fond of you." From those stories I probably sounded like any teenage girl's father's nightmare.

"But I know your folks. I know what great people they are. And I know you've been through a lot, too. So I tried to just chalk your behavior up to you going through an understandably rough time and just being young and foolish."

I want to say something. That he's right. That I was young and foolish and going through a really rough time, but he continues before I can say anything.

"Even as my girls have gotten older I've overheard more tales about you, and they haven't improved my opinion of you at all." My heart sinks. I can imagine the things Robert overheard about me from Callie and Jules, and I should probably just see myself to the door.

"But recently I've seen you stepping up in ways that I never expected. And I've been overhearing some different stories about you that have made me wonder about you. If maybe you're a different man than you once were." I feel the smallest spark of hope that maybe Robert isn't going to chase me out of his house with a shotgun.

"I've seen how you are with Evie, and that has made me wonder if I should reassess my assumptions about you. For some reason Jules seems to trust you, and she always has good judgment. But my trust isn't given, Jacob. It's earned." Robert gives me a hard look, daring me to respond.

"I understand, sir, and I hope I can earn your trust. And I hope you know that's important to me, because..." I hear Jules coming down the stairs; I stop what I'm saying mid-sentence, unable to finish my thought, unable to explain myself to Robert.

Jules walks into the living room. "What have you two rascals been talking about?" she asks, plopping onto the opposite side of the couch I'm sitting on. She looks between the two of us a bit nervously. She's seemed a bit tense tonight; I never should have mentioned anything to her about her dad not liking me.

"Oh, just guy stuff. Sports," her dad says, smiling. *Sports, bars, and sports bars*, I chuckle to myself. "And Jacob offered to help me with the fence repair."

"He did?" Jules asks, surprised. Just as surprised as I am that I've apparently offered to help with a fence repair that I've never even heard mentioned. "You don't have to do that. My dad and I can handle it," she says a bit nervously, fiddling with the zipper on the oversized hoodie she's wearing that I recognize as Dylan's.

I know this is a test, that Robert wants to see if I'll put the work in to earn his trust. "I know you can," I say smiling at Jules. "But I want to help, and it doesn't hurt to have an extra set of hands."

Jules smiles brightly at me. "OK, that will be a big help. Thanks, Jake. You're the best."

Robert catches my eye and gives me a look that I take to mean *Prove it.*

CHAPTER 14

Jake

I am thrilled when Jules invited me to meet her and Evie at a park after work one day. Jules and I walk a path around the park while Evie goes bonkers on the playground in the middle of the park; we keep an eye on her while we stroll. I keep glancing at Jules out of the corner of my eye, admiring how good she looks in the simple blue dress she wore to work today. I chuckle to myself thinking there are probably a few five-year-old boys who have a little crush on Ms. Nelson. Then I start thinking maybe there are a few dads from the elementary school who have a little crush on Ms. Nelson, too.

"What?" Jules asks, and I realize I've been staring while lost in thought.

Oh nothing, just spiraling over here worrying that some single dad is going to fall in love with you and I'll attend your wedding as a guest for the second time.

I shake myself from my unwelcome thoughts. "I wanted to ask you, can I borrow Evie Thursday afternoon?"

"Um excuse me? *Borrow* my daughter? What is this like the new 'getting a dog to attract women' scheme but now instead of a dog it's a child?

"Jesus, Jules, no!" I exclaim indignantly. *Is she just joking or does she really think I would do something like that?*

"Then what are you *borrowing* her for?" she asks skeptically.

"My parents want to have her over to play."

"Really?" Jules smiles brightly. "That's sweet of them."

"I think it's finally dawned on them that they're never getting grandchildren," I answer hesitantly, rubbing my neck as I explain. "And they've decided my goddaughter is their only chance at getting to fawn over an adorable little kid."

Jules gives me a look that almost looks like pity then shakes her head at me. *Was that pity for me or my parents?*

"Your parents are the best," Jules says with a sweet smile. I completely agree. My parents are the absolute best. I feel guilty all the time for what I put them through during my wrecking ball teenager stage; they didn't need me to add anything to their plate, and I really heaped it on.

"Evie can definitely go with you to play at your parents' house Thursday, and she will gladly soak up all of their fawning. What time should I drop her off?" Jules asks.

I have to take a deep breath to gather my courage to ask her my next question. "Do you want to come, too? I know my mom would love a chance to catch up with you." I know she and Jules could talk for hours about school, and I think my mom would guilt trip me endlessly if I didn't invite Jules. Plus, I can't deny that I also want to invite Jules just for me.

"Do *I* want to come?" Jules asks, seemingly surprised by the invitation. I wait as she thinks over my offer, trying not to look too hopeful. "Sure that'd be great."

"And stay for dinner, too. I know they'll insist."

"OK. What can I bring?" she asks, thoughtful as always.

"Nothing just yourself and your adorable daughter."

"No, I can't just show up empty handed and expect your family to feed me. I'll call your mom and see what I can bring."

Call my mom? I stop in my tracks. "Wait, do you have my mom's number?" I ask surprised.

"Of course, I do," Jules says nonchalantly stopping just a few feet in front of me.

"How? Why?" I sputter unable to move.

"She reached out to me when I started working in the school district."

"Oh," I say quietly, resuming walking. "Do you… do you talk to her often?" *Shit what have I said to my mom that she's repeated to Jules without me knowing it?*

"Occasionally. But we don't talk about you if that's what you're so worried about," Jules says, like she's reading my mind. "Or at least we don't *only* talk about you," she says grinning at me.

I open my parents' front door before Jules and Evie reach the porch. "Hey, sweet pea," I say, wrapping Evie in a hug and carrying her into the house. "Oh, and hey Jules," I say as an afterthought over my shoulder. She smiles and shakes her head at me.

Jules is soon ambushed by my mother who hugs her, takes the salad from her hands and fusses over how she didn't need to bring anything. My dad gives Jules a quick hug, his blue eyes twinkling in a way that is a giveaway that he's as charmed by her as ever.

"Evie these are my parents, Debbie and John," I say introducing Evie to my parents. My mom and dad smile at her kindly. Evie waves shyly and tucks her head into my shoulder.

"Meeting new people makes me feel shy, too," my dad says. "There's something in the back yard I think you'll like, Evie." We follow him to the back yard toward the swing hanging between two trees. Evie's eyes light up.

Jules walks up beside me and whispers, "I played on that swing, Jake. How old are those ropes?"

"New ropes, Jules dear. I just hung it up again this week," my dad says, apparently having overheard Jules's question.

"Just checking. Sorry, John," Jules says, cheeks slightly pink.

"That's your job, Mom," my dad says smiling at Jules.

Within a few minutes Evie has completely warmed up to my parents and is talking their ears off telling them some endless story about playing cats with her friends at recess. My parents are enthralled, and Jules looks amused.

While my dad and I see to the grill outside, my mom and Jules go inside with Evie to play with some toys my mom bought specifically for today. She didn't have a daughter, so she maybe went a little overboard with shopping for little girl toys. Through the sliding glass door, I watch the scene unfold: as my mom brings out more and more toys she and Evie become more and more excited while Jules becomes more and more overwhelmed. I slide the door open a crack. "Mom, that's probably enough toys to bring out this visit," I warn gently. My mom gives me a thumbs up and she and Evie continue playing.

I catch Jules's eye and she mouths, *"Thank you,"* giving me a grateful smile.

I turn around to see my dad staring at me with a small grin on his face, blue eyes sparkling with excitement. "This visit, huh?" he says a little too excitedly.

"Well, Evie is my goddaughter. I hope I'll be able to bring her over more often," I say a bit evasively.

He gives me a knowing look that I ignore, busying myself with checking the grill.

Jules

Evie is having a blast playing with Debbie, and I am having a great time, too. It is so funny watching Debbie go just as nuts as Evie over the pony toys, pink and purple building blocks, and other supposedly 'girly' toys Debbie bought for the occasion. I get my fill of this kind of play any day of the week, so I enjoy myself watching Debbie and Evie play while gabbing away with Debbie.

She is always so fun. At the few work meetings we have attended together, Debbie has had me in stitches the entire time. I love John to pieces, but Jake definitely gets his sense of humor from his mom.

She's so fun, so warm. When I'm talking with Debbie it feels almost like talking with my sister Callie – we can talk for hours about almost anything. When she asks me questions – about work, where I get my hair done, my favorite park in town – I feel like she's really interested, like she's really listening to me. I am aware that I can talk, so I am always grateful to have someone willing to listen.

Debbie's the kind of mom I wish I had and the kind of mom I want to be. It's not hard to outshine my own mother, obviously, but even disregarding my own mother's poor example, Debbie has always stood out to me as a wonderful mom.

When I met Dylan I had this small, ridiculous hope that his mom and I would become close. That my mother-in-law could in some ways fill in for my own absent-by-choice mother. I don't know if Laurel's and my strained relationship had anything to do with it, but in the ten years Dylan I were together, and in the time since, Ellen and I have never become close. And in all that time I've barely even gotten to know Dylan's father Michael. There have been so many times I thought we would grow closer – when planning Dylan's and my wedding, when Evie was born, even during the months of Dylan's illness. I was disappointed but not surprised that she never did come over from Redmond to help Evie and me after Dylan passed.

I'm trying to keep in mind that every family is different, every family shows they care in different ways. But sometimes it's really hard to feel like Dylan's family cares about me or even about Evie. I have never felt welcome or like I'm a part of the Bailey family. And I have had to basically force Evie on them the past few months so that she knows who they are, knows her dad's family, the people she shares a name with.

Sitting here in Debbie and John's living room, seeing how easily Evie is bonding with them, knowing that they make me feel at ease, welcome, home, it seems like this is how it should be. *How* what *should be?* I suddenly think, shaking myself from my strange reverie.

Jake

Over dinner, Evie tells a *riveting* story about playing chase with one of her friends at recess, and my parents are hanging on her every word. I see Jules zoning out as the story goes on and on; she probably hears some version of this story every day. I notice something in the corner of the room grabs her attention and I realize she's spotted my dad's guitar. I lean over and ask her quietly, "Do you want to play after dinner?" inclining my head toward the guitar.

Jules frowns. "Maybe next time," she answers, tucking a stray curl behind her ear and turning her attention to Evie.

I nod, concerned that I've upset her. But then I can't stop myself from replaying her words in my head. *Next time.*

The five of us have had a wonderful evening. Evie has had such a great time she starts crying when she and Jules have to leave, which nearly brings my mom to tears, too. After a few hugs and promises that she can come back to swing and play any time, Evie finally allows me to carry her to Jules's car. Proudly she holds out the sketch I drew of her swinging, and tells Jules, "I want to hang this in my room." Jules gives me a look over Evie's head and I have to bite the inside of my cheek to stop myself from laughing.

I buckle Evie into her booster seat and give her a kiss on the forehead goodnight. I turn to Jules and feel myself overcome with the urge to give her a kiss goodnight, too, but I settle for a friendly hug instead.

"Thank you for tonight, Jake," she says looking up at me, her dark eyes reflecting the light of the streetlamps, arms still wrapped around my waist. "Evie had such a wonderful time and so did I. Your parents are amazing. You're such a great guy, and we're both so lucky to have you."

I want to tell her, *I'm the lucky one.* But I can't bring myself to say it out loud. My heart pounding, I manage to say, "Thank you for coming over tonight and for making my parents' month, Jules. Have a good night."

"Night, Jake."

"Night, Jake!" Evie echoes.

After watching Jules's car disappear into the night I head back inside. My parents are sitting in the living room, and I can tell they are waiting to interrogate me. I barely have a chance to sit down before my mom starts. "Please tell me there's something going on between you and Jules," she says, barely able to conceal the excitement in her voice.

I let out a breath. "I don't know, Mom," I answer honestly. "I don't know if she sees me that way."

"Well what about you? What are you feeling?"

"We both know you already know the answer to that question, Mom."

~~~

I stood at the bar ordering another drink, taking my time talking to the pretty bartender. Dylan walked up and slapped a hand on my shoulder. "Hey, Jake, we're going to do the toasts now. Are you ready?"

"Just need one more shot of liquid courage, then I'll be ready," I said raising my shot glass and downing it with a wink at the bartender.

"OK, great," Dylan said steering me away from the bar, probably worried I might indulge in a few more rounds of liquid courage before giving my best man speech. "You'll go after Callie."

Callie delivered a sweet matron of honor speech about how lucky she was growing up with a sister like Jules. There were a few tearful moments that the guests completely ate up. As Callie handed me the microphone she hissed, "Behave, Jacob." What is it with those Nelson girls thinking I can't behave myself? *I thought to myself. I winked at her, and I could tell she really didn't want to hand over the microphone. She finally relented.*

"For those of you who don't know me, I'm Dylan's good for nothing college roommate, Jake."

The crowd of wedding guests offered a low rumble of laughter.

"As Dylan's roommate, I had a front row seat - or maybe a top bunk seat," I said making a face, my quip earning another laugh from the crowd. I saw Dylan shake his head laughing and Jules duck her head, tucking into Dylan's shoulder out of amusement and a touch of embarrassment. "A top bunk seat to Dylan and Jules's love story unfolding. And it truly has been
~~~

a fairy tale." That comment earned a chorus of 'aww' from the guests. "It really has been a joy to see these two incredible people falling in love and building a life together."

I cleared my throat before continuing. "I want to raise a toast to my best friend. The person who makes me want to be a better man. Who has been by my side through some of the most difficult and most incredible times of my life. Today I'm happy knowing you are with the person who was meant for you. I wish you both every happiness in the world." I raised my glass and the guests raised their glasses in suit. "Cheers!"

As I brought my glass to my lips, my eyes drifted across the room, landing on my mom. She looked at me with such sadness and pity, I realized she was the only other person in the room who knew I hadn't been talking about Dylan.

~~~

"Whatever happens, I'm glad Evie and Jules are part of your life," my mom says kindly.

"Me too, Mom," I say with what I hope is a convincing smile. *But I don't think that's enough for me anymore. And I don't really know where to go from here.*
~~~

CHAPTER 15

Jake

"Are you hungry?" I ask Jules when we're a few minutes from town, on our way back from the mountain.

"Always," Jules answers.

I grin at her completely honest response. "Do you want to get a bite to eat downtown?" I ask. I've been planning all week to ask her to dinner, trying to come up with the perfect way to nonchalantly invite her out.

"Downtown? Dressed like this?" Jules asks incredulously, gesturing to her long johns and fleece pullover.

"Good point, bad idea" I say laughing, trying not to sound disappointed.

"But if you give me 20 minutes, I can get changed and meet you downtown," Jules says, instantly perking me up again. "Evie's in Redmond until tomorrow morning, so I have the night to myself. Dinner downtown sounds fun."

"You have a kid-free night? In that case you shouldn't have to drive. You might want to hit that wine bar again," I tease, grinning at her.

"No. No, I won't," Jules says adamantly. "It turns out kids don't understand hangovers," she says wincing I'm guessing at the memory of the aftermath of her last wine bar visit.

"Wine bar or not, I'll pick you up. I'll swing by in half an hour."

"OK, that will be great," she says excitedly.

I hold the door to the restaurant open, taking the opportunity to admire Jules walking past me. She's a knockout even in ski gear and oversized men's t-shirts, but tonight, in her blouse and tight jeans, I'm having trouble not gawking at her.

When we step into the restaurant, we hear someone call, "Jules!" I see Jules's face light up as she spots the tall blonde at a nearby table. Jules walks toward the table where her sister Callie and her husband Ryan are sitting. Callie jumps up, meeting Jules halfway and wraps her in a tight hug; they both make a fuss over how great it is to run into each other, as if they don't see each other almost every other day. Jules and Callie look a lot alike – both blond, the same brown eyes, both athletic, though Callie is a little taller with straight hair. And, of course, they're both gorgeous and drawing the attention of half the restaurant; their dad must have been a nervous wreck through their teen years.

Callie looks over Jules's shoulder as she asks, "Who are you here with?"

"Just Jake," I hear Jules answer, and I feel myself deflate at that explanation. *Just Jake. Will she ever see me as more than* Just Jake? I groan to myself. "We're grabbing some dinner after being on the mountain all day."

Callie gives me a critical look, then smiles, though the smile doesn't reach her eyes. "We just sat down," she says, pointing to the table where Ryan waves lamely at us. "You should join us."

After some moving of drinks, I find myself sitting next to Jules on the other side of the table from Callie and Ryan. Jules and Callie gab away about everything and anything, from skiing to psychology. I don't know Ryan too well, but we end up finding a few safe topics – mostly hiking and the Seahawks. *Sports, bars, and sports bars*, I chuckle to myself. At one point in our conversation I unconsciously rest my arm on the back of Jules's chair. I physically feel the piercing look that Callie gives me and drop my arm as if the chairback is on fire.

Partway through our meal, Callie excuses herself to the restroom. A few minutes later I do the same. I make my way down the hallway to the men's restroom. Halfway down the hall someone steps in front of me, intentionally blocking my path.

"Callie," I say grinning. "Just what you've always wanted. Me, alone in a dark hallway."

"Jacob, what are you doing?" Callie asks, ignoring my lewd joke and speaking to me like I'm a misbehaving child.

"Exactly what it looks like I'm doing," I say pointing to the door of the men's room.

"Not what I mean and you know it," she says giving me a hard look. "What are you doing? Jules. You. Dinner. What are you doing?"

"Exactly what it looks like I'm doing," I repeat, grumbling.

"Which is what?" Callie asks, her eyes narrowing in the same way Jules's do when she's winding up for a lecture. Robert, Callie, Jules – lecturing must be a family trait.

"You tell me. What does it look like I'm doing, Callie?" I huff.

"If I didn't know any better I'd say it looks like you're on a date with my sister."

"And that's exactly what I'm doing," I say nonchalantly and try to brush past Callie.

She slams her hand into my shoulder, stopping me.

"You're what?!" she gasps, the shocked look on her face is so absurd it would almost be funny if her surprise weren't so unnerving. *Why does she look so horrified? Would Jules dating me really be so awful?* I ask myself.

"You heard me," I snap, starting to lose my temper. "Now if you'll excuse me I came back here for a reason and it wasn't to be interrogated by you."

Callie's jaw snaps shut, and she gives me a determined look. She grabs my arm and drags me through a back entrance to the alleyway behind the restaurant.

"She's my sister; I get to interrogate you all I want," she snarls at me once we're outside. Callie's right. I lean up against the wall, resigned. I wave my hands toward myself as if to say *Fire away*. "You two are together? She never told me…"

"No, no, no, Callie, it's not like that," I say hurriedly, panicking that Callie has made some leaps and bounds of assumptions. And I realize my annoyed, cryptic answer definitely sent her in that direction. "We're not together… I mean not yet…I mean I hope…" I stumble over my words. "I thought maybe tonight if we had dinner just the two of us it would turn into more of a date, and then we ran into you and…" I rub the back of my neck and look at Callie helplessly.

Callie gapes at me. Then a smug smile slowly spreads across her face. "I never thought I'd see the day," she says shaking her head, completely amused.

"What?" I snap at her.

"Jake Thompson. Hopelessly in love," she says smirking. "I never thought I'd see the day," she repeats. I scowl at her, but I don't deny it. "I always had my suspicions, though, about how you felt about her. Way back when," she says, tapping her chin thoughtfully. "I think everyone did. Except maybe Jules."

Good. If there's anyone I didn't want to know that I've spent so many years of my life pining away after Jules, it's Jules.

"Well where does Jules stand on all of this?" Callie asks.

"What do you mean?"

"How does Jules feel about you?" she asks slowly, her tone just on the edge of condescending.

I shake my head. "I honestly don't know."

Callie blinks at me. "There's a pretty easy way to find out the answer," she says in a patronizing voice. "You could ask her." Callie tilts her head, assessing the look of terror on my face just from the idea of asking Jules how she feels about me. "Or we could act like we're in middle school again and I could ask her for you," she says grinning at me and ruffling my hair, like I'm 12.

I swat her hand away. "I'm not ready to talk to her about it. I just need some more time. Let things simmer a bit longer. Give the ole' Jake Thompson charm a little more time to do its magic."

"No," Callie says flatly, crossing her arms in front of her chest. "I know the *ole' Jake Thompson charm*. And if that's what you're up to my dad and I will arm wrestle over who gets to turn the shotgun on you."

I raise my hands placatingly. "That's not what I meant. OK, the *new* Jake Thompson charm."

"And what is the *new* Jake Thompson charm?" Callie asks skeptically.

"This," I say pointing between the two of us. "Letting you interrogate me in this alleyway. Spending a whole day re-building a fence with your dad and letting him interrogate me whenever Jules was out of earshot. Watching Evie on a Friday night so Jules can go out with her friends. Trying to prove that I might actually be worthy of her."

"Prove it to who?" Callie asks meaningfully.

"To her," I answer. *And maybe to me, too.*

Callie regards me, resting a finger on her cheek. "I'm not saying you've won me over yet, because you haven't. I've known you too long. I know all the crap you've done. All of it." I close my eyes and sigh, because I know how Jules and Callie talk, and I'm sure Callie knows more about me than anyone should. "But maybe I need to get to know the *new* Jake Thompson." She gives me a half smile that I mirror back at her.

Callie gives me an unexpected, quick hug that I return awkwardly before we turn to head back into the restaurant. As I hold the service door open, Callie rests her hand on my arm, giving me a concerned look.

"And Jake? Just talk to her."

"Sure," I mutter, knowing full well that I won't.

Jules

On Tuesday Callie and Ryan come over for their weekly dinner with Evie, my dad, and me. While Callie and I work in the kitchen to prepare dinner we chat, like we always do, about everything under the sun - our work weeks so far, what her friends are up to these days, our favorite brand of salsa, you name it.

"So have you been on any more dates since that one guy?" Callie asks, offhandedly. "What was his name?"

I chuckle to myself going through a long list of possible answers. "I can't remember. And no, I haven't. That one date was such a disaster I haven't had the nerve to try again. Not that I've even had the opportunity to try again. There's not exactly a long line of men just waiting to take me out," I joke.

Callie's forehead wrinkles like she's thinking about something. She opens her mouth like she's going to say something then snaps her mouth shut again, more forehead wrinkles appearing.

"What?" I ask.

"Nothing," Callie answers reflexively, a dead giveaway that she's not telling me something. She busies herself by tossing the green salad, the green salad she already tossed five minutes ago.

My eyes narrow at her. "Seriously, what?" I ask again. She shakes her head silently. "There's obviously something you want to say. Will you just tell me?"

Callie turns to me, with a wary look on her face. She opens her mouth, but a timer goes off letting me know the lasagna in the oven is ready. Callie uses the distraction as an opportunity to slip out of the kitchen. I mutter to myself, *She's just going to tell me eventually anyway,* and try to ignore my curiosity and the nagging feeling that I probably need to know whatever she isn't telling me.

CHAPTER 16

Jake

Jules and I are riding the lift up to take one last run before we head home. It has been a perfect spring ski day.

"What a perfect day," Jules says, her words echoing my thoughts completely.

"I know. We've been so lucky to be able to ski so late into the season. You couldn't ask for better spring conditions," I say.

"Or better company," Jules says, knocking me with her shoulder playfully. I grin back at her and when our eyes meet I feel a familiar pull to her.

"You're always faster than me, so go ahead and I'll meet you back at the car," Jules says as she adjusts her gloves and ski poles once we're off the lift.

"Are you sure?" I ask. I always feel guilty leaving her behind so I usually wait for her at the bottom of each run.

"Yes, I'm sure," she giggles. "We probably only have one more weekend after today, so I want to enjoy it. At my own pace, without feeling guilty that I'm holding you up."

"You don't hold me up," I fib, just a little.

"You are a terrible liar," Jules laughs. "Get going, hot shot," she says shoving my chest lightly.

The way she's been flirting with me, the sun lighting up her blond curls, the giant smile on her face – it all gives me the courage to do something I've wanted to do for weeks now. I grab the hand that she shoved me with, pull her toward me, and kiss her.

For an instant everything is perfect. We're perfect, like two puzzle pieces snapping into place. Then Jules rears back and gasps, "What the hell was that?" She stares at me, eyes wide with shock.

I stare back just as shocked by her reaction, astounded by my own idiocy. How had I deluded myself into thinking she felt the same way I did? I can't bear the wave of disappointment that hits me. I don't say a word, turning and taking off down the slope.

"Jake, wait!" I hear Jules calling after me. "Jake! Stop! Jacob!"

I don't turn back. I can't outrun the fucking enormous mistake I just made, but I can outrun her. Because she was right. I am faster than her.

Jules

Jake is already waiting in the driver's seat when I approach his car. I open the lift gate, take off my helmet, change out of my boots, and put my gear away. Jake doesn't even turn around. He doesn't acknowledge me in the slightest. I crawl into the passenger seat, and Jake still doesn't even look at me. "Hey," I say quietly.

"Hey," he says flatly, starting the engine and pulling out of the parking spot.

"I'm sorry about the way I reacted up there. You just... I was just... I wasn't expecting that. I was caught off guard, and –"

"Just stop," Jake says, cutting me off. I stop talking, waiting for him to say something else, but he doesn't say another word.

My patience wearing, I start again, "Jake, please let's just talk about –"

"Jules! I said stop! Just stop!" he shouts cutting me off again. "There is nothing to talk about."

I gape at him. "Yes, there is! You can't just pretend like nothing happened up there," I snap in disbelief, gesturing to the general direction of the mountain top. The mountain top where, to my complete shock, he just kissed me.

Jake clenches his jaw, grips the steering wheel harder, straightens his broad shoulders, but he doesn't say another word.

I throw my hands up defeated and turn in my seat to stare out the passenger window in silence. Neither of us utters another word for the rest of the drive.

We arrive at my dad's house, and I open the passenger door wordlessly. I have so much gear to bring in – skis, ski boots, helmet, ski jacket, backpack – it will take me at least two trips to get all of my things to the house. And all I can think is how embarrassing it is going to be for me to see Jake just sitting in his car, not talking to me, while I make *two* trips back and forth from his car. I'm surprised when Jake steps out of the car and wordlessly grabs half of my gear. He walks beside me and delivers my things to the front door in silence. I can't tell if he wanted to help or he just wanted to get away from me that much faster.

"Jake," I say quietly, hating the undertone of pleading in my voice. He ignores me and returns to his car in silence. Feeling both unbearably frustrated and infuriatingly helpless I watch him climb into his car and drive away.

What the hell was that? The words echo in my head. *What the hell was that?*

I flop onto my bed and bury my head under my pillows.

Where did that come from? Jake and I have always been friends. Just friends. I know he's never seen me as anything more. Way back when I thought there might be something more between us, he made damn sure I knew that we were just friends.

~~~

Jake walked up to me in the hall during the passing period between classes. "Hey! You haven't signed my yearbook yet," he said holding his yearbook out to me. I took his yearbook and handed him mine, glancing at the clock.
~~~

"I have to get to English class right now, so I can't sign it this instant." I had a test and wanted to review my notes. *"Can I give it to you in calc class?"* We had calculus together the next period, so I wouldn't have his yearbook too long, but I would have enough time to write his note.

"That'll work. But don't lose mine," he said with false reproach.

I rolled my eyes. *"Don't lose mine,"* I grumbled.

I finished my English test with a few minutes to spare in the class period, so I was able to write a note in Jake's yearbook. It wasn't too lengthy, but it was heartfelt. I told him that it had been a joy to grow up with him, how proud I was of him, and that I was excited to be at U of O together the next year.

Once we were in the calc classroom, Jake and I returned each other's yearbooks. Immediately another friend asked for my yearbook, so I didn't get a chance to see what Jake had written until she handed it back to me half-way through class.

Jules,
Thanks for always being a great friend.
Go Ducks!
Jake
Underneath his signature he drew a little Oregon Duck cartoon figure.

That's it? I wanted to scream. One sentence that could have been written to just about anybody in our graduating class. Once again, his message was loud and clear. For the past two years Jake had made it unavoidably clear that, to him, I was nothing more than a friend. And apparently, even after everything we had been through together, an insignificant friend at that.

I was suddenly embarrassed that I had written something that I thought was meaningful in his yearbook. I cringed recalling my signature 'Through anything, Your Jules.' I was overcome with the urge to rip the note I had written him out of his yearbook and tear it into a thousand pieces before he could even read it.

Jake was sitting on the other side of the classroom from me; out of the *corner of my eye I noticed him reading from his yearbook, and I could only assume he was reading the mortifying note I had written. I saw him glance at me, but I was determined not to look at him. I didn't want to know if he felt guilty or embarrassed or if he was cringing at the way I poured my heart out on his yearbook page or if he was laughing at me. I didn't want to know, because if I wanted to know it meant I cared. And I couldn't care about what Jake did or what he thought of me. I couldn't care that he dated my friends and never missed a chance to give me a front-row view to all of his romantic escapades.*

At the end of class I bolted for the door while trying to look nonchalant about it. Jake still caught up with me in the hallway, hustling into position beside me, slowing his long strides to match my own.

"Hey, Jules, can I … uh… see your yearbook again?" Jake asked rubbing the back of his neck in her nervous way as he walked beside me.

No. There is no way I am giving him my yearbook so he can write some bullshit P.S. out of pity or guilt, *I growled to myself.*

Fortunately I had stuffed my yearbook into my backpack before I fled the math classroom. "There are a bunch of people I want to sign it in my next class, so maybe later," I replied, determined to be indifferent. Jake frowned and opened his mouth to say something. "Cute Fighting Duck, though. Thanks," I said, with what I hoped looked like a real smile, cutting him off before he could even start. I picked up my pace and walked away as quickly as I could manage, resolved to not look back and trying to stay calm when my instinct was urging me to run.

~~~

Head still buried under my pillows, my confused thoughts return to the matter at hand. *What brought this* incident *about? Was it some spontaneous I-haven't-gotten-laid-in-a-long-time-and-you're-a-female-within-arm's-reach instinctive reaction? Or is there something else going on? Jake has given me no indication that anything has changed between us. Or has he? Am I really that dense that I wouldn't notice? Did I miss some kind of clue that –* My thoughts stop abruptly.

"Callie," I growl aloud. I toss my pillow aside, snatch up my phone, and immediately dial her number, already fuming by the
~~~

time the call connects.

"Hi, JuJu," Callie answers her phone sweetly, using the name she has used for me since we were kids, back when the *s* sound in *Jules* was hard for her.

"Hello, Callista," I say, my voice icy. It's hard not being able to pronounce the s sound when your name is *Callista*. That's one reason why she's always gone by Callie. Unless she's in trouble. Which she is right now. Callie doesn't respond right away, sensing my foul mood.

"What is it Jules? Why are you calling me?"

"I've had the most interesting afternoon," I say, trying to stay calm. "And it occurred to me just now that you withheld a very important piece of information from me the other night."

"Jules, I can tell you're upset. What happened?" she asks, and I hear the concern in her voice.

"And," I carry on as if I haven't heard her, "if you hadn't withheld that information I wouldn't have made such a fucking fool of myself today."

There's a long pause before she responds. "Jules, if this is about what I think it's about, that wasn't my secret to tell."

"What secret? What is going on?" I hear my voice raising. "For God's sake why won't anyone just talk to me?" I shout.

"I'm coming over. Right now," Callie snaps into the phone and the line goes dead. I flop onto my bed wallowing in confusion and frustration. *What secret? What does Callie know that I don't?*

A few minutes later I hear Callie unlock the front door. She strides down the hall and flops down on the bed next to me. She props herself up on her elbows, a small grin on her face. I scowl at the ceiling. *Why does this feel like we're in high school again?*

"You want to talk, so let's talk," Callie says the grin on her face broadening. She seems like she is enjoying this. I don't say anything, still fuming. "Spill the tea, Jules," she says shaking my arm. "Don't keep me in suspense. Whatever happened it's got to be good if it has you this riled up."

"Incorrigible gossip," I mutter making Callie grin. I sigh loudly. "Jake kissed me," I say flatly.

Callie blinks at me, shockingly *not* shocked by my news. "And?" Callie prods me.

"And…" I echo. "And I wasn't expecting it. At all. And I didn't have the best reaction…"

"What did you do?" Callie asks, with a look of concern.

I close my eyes, haunted by my own thoughtless words. "I said… I said, 'What the hell was that?'"

"Ouch," Callie says grimacing. *Ugh 'ouch' is right.*

"And you should have seen the look on his face," I groan, rubbing my eyes trying to erase that image from my memory. "It was like I slapped him. And then he just took off. Down the mountain without even looking back. I tried to apologize but he wouldn't let me and he wouldn't talk to me. And he just dropped me here, and I don't understand what the hell just happened.

"But I remembered you the other night," I turn to Callie with what I hope is a withering gaze. "How tight-lipped you were, that you were clearly keeping something from me. So I thought now that I've made such a disaster of everything you might enlighten me."

Callie squirms. "He didn't say anything? At all?" she asks with discomfort.

"No. Nothing. Not a word. The only thing he said was 'There's nothing to talk about.' Like, really? Nothing to talk about? Are you kidding me? And I can't figure out if he's just being his usual *Jake Thompson Ladies' Man Extraordinaire*-self and I was the only woman in his proximity or if maybe it was…something else."

Could there be something else happening that I've just been too dense to pick up on? But what else could it be?

Callie considers my words, pursing her lips, seemingly mulling something over. "It's something else, Jules," she says softly.

"Then what is it? What are you not telling me? Jake and I have been friends for so long and he never took any interest whatsoever. He took an interest in every other girl within arm's reach but never me, and…" I stop when I see the pained look on Callie's face. "What?"

"Have you never wondered if maybe with how close you two

were that there was a reason he never got involved with you?"

I roll my eyes. "I know the reason. Complete lack of interest." *Obviously. I was just the only girl who could never turn his head.*

Callie shakes her head at me. "He's always been crazy about you, Jules."

"What?" I gasp. "That's impossible." *That's impossible, right? He's messed around with every girl with a pulse but he never took any interest in me whatsoever. Because he just wasn't interested. At all. Right?*

"Look, I don't want to say anything else. I told Jake he needed to talk to you, which he obviously didn't do. I couldn't just sit here seeing you in misery and leave you completely in the dark, but if you want to know anything else you need to talk to Jake."

And he won't talk to me. Great.

"But before you talk to him, maybe you need to do some self-reflection," Callie says earnestly.

"Self-reflection?"

"Yeah. Think about how you feel. What you want."

Oh. I stare blankly at Callie. *What do I want?*

If I think about it we have been spending a lot of time together recently. And some of our teasing has become more playful, almost, well, flirty. And maybe there has been more, I guess, physical affection between us. And I know I've felt myself blush a few times when his eye has caught mine. And something about that kiss, before I freaked out, felt almost…right. And… Oh my God. Have I been falling for Jake?

CHAPTER 17

Jules

I try calling Jake a few times over the next few days, but he ignores my calls. He has the audacity to send me a message on Wednesday, the same message he has been sending me almost every Wednesday for the past few months.

JAKE: Are we going skiing this weekend?

Is he serious? Sending that casual message like nothing happened. Like I haven't been trying to get him to talk to me for the past five days. Talk to me about how he kissed *me.*

JULES: Are we going to talk about what happened at the top of that run?
JAKE: No
JULES: Then no

If Jake is going to be childish and unwilling to talk to me about whatever the hell happened at the top of that ski run, then I can be just as childish. *Enjoy skiing by yourself, Jacob,* I growl to myself. It's the last weekend of the ski season, and even though I'm disappointed to miss it, I can't be around Jake if he won't talk to me about what happened at the top of that run.

On Sunday morning my phone lights up with a call from Jake. *Maybe he's finally willing to talk about what happened,* I think to myself. *Doubt it,* I grumble.

"Good morning, Jacob," I say formally.

"Jules, dear?" I hear a woman's voice say. *Oh my God why is Jake's mom calling me? And on Jake's phone?* I ask myself, my heart filling with dread.

"Debbie? Is everything OK?"

"Well, dear…Jake had an accident on the mountain yesterday."

Ice grips my heart. *Not again.* "Oh my God. Is he…?" I start to ask.

"It's fine dear, everything's fine. He'll be alright," she says hurriedly, realizing that I'm imagining the worst.

"What happened?" I ask, trying to stay calm.

"Took a tumble and snapped his collarbone." I let out a breath. *It's just his collarbone. Thank God.* "Nothing that a little time and patience and whole lot of pain won't fix. But I thought you should know."

"Is he at your place?" I ask, thinking his parents are probably taking care of him.

"No, he insisted we take him back to his house. And he's being pretty stubborn. Says he can take care of himself." *Stubborn idiot,* I growl to myself.

"That's actually why I called," Debbie continues. "I told him I'd leave once he was asleep, but I haven't wanted to leave him by himself. I hoped he might be more receptive to you checking in on him."

I'm not too sure about that, I grumble to myself. "I'll head over there now, Debbie," I say already rushing around trying to find my purse and a pair of shoes.

"Thank you, Jules dear. I… I know you mean a lot to him," she says tentatively.

I don't know how to respond to that. "I'll see you in a few minutes. And Debbie?"

"Yes, dear?"

"Just so you know you're using Jake's phone." *And you just scared the shit out of me by calling me from it.*

"Oh shoot? I am?" she laughs loudly. "This looks just like mine. Thanks for telling me. He would have been so mad if I'd walked out of here with his phone."

I walk into the living room where my dad and Evie are playing with Duplos and wave my dad into the other room so I can tell him what's going on without alarming Evie.

"Go, go, we're fine," my dad says, practically pushing me out the door as soon as I fill him in. "Take care of Jake. He needs you," he says, giving me a meaningful look that I ignore. *Jeez. Callie, Debbie, my dad… Am I the only one who was surprised by what happened on the top of that run?*

"I'll try to be back in time to make dinner," I say.

"Don't worry about dinner. I'll cook," he offers. *I bet he'll make pot roast, I think, making a silent bet with myself.* "I'll make a pot roast," he says proudly, and I have to bite the inside of my cheek so I don't laugh out loud.

Jake

I wake up and instinctively try to roll over on my side, which makes me cry out in pain. Through blurry eyes I see someone kneeling next to me. For an instant I guess it must be my mom, and I'm annoyed that she didn't leave like I asked her to. But then my vision comes into focus and I realize it's probably the last person I want to see me like this. "What are you doing here?" I grumble.

"I was making a log for the medications you're taking, but then I heard you howl, so I came in here to see what you needed," Jules answers, her voice clipped.

"A log? So professional," I mutter sarcastically.

"I've had plenty of practice," she says flatly. I still at her words. In the months that Dylan was sick I'm sure she did have plenty of practice.

Our eyes meet. "You shouldn't have to do this," I huff.

"Do what?" she asks.

"Take care of me." *I'm supposed to be the one taking care of you,* I grumble to myself. "You have enough responsibilities without having to worry about me. Thanks for checking on me, but I'm fine. Really," I say, trying to sit up, but the pain is too great and I give up with a frustrated sigh.

Jules sits down on the bed. "I'll leave if you want me to. Your mom asked me to come check on you so I did. And I wanted to be sure you were OK."

"She what?" I ask horrified. *Why would my mom ask Jules to check on me?*

"She's worried about you, you jerk!" Jules exclaims, her eyes narrowing. "Why would you run her off like that? And after everything she's been through…" Jules trails off, looking away, her eyes filling with tears.

No! Why is she crying again? I can't take it when she cries. Instinctively I reach over with my good arm and take Jules's hand. Her eyes turn to my hand on hers. She takes a shaky breath. "When your mom called and said you had been in a ski accident all I could think was, '*Not again,*'" she explains, her voice hoarse with emotion.

I hate to think what Jules must have felt getting that call; Jules had good reason to fear the worst.

~~~

A whole group of kids from our high school were heading up to the mountain for the day. Johnny, my older brother, drove Callie, Jules, and me while his friends drove in another car. Johnny and Callie and all the others were seniors, while Jules and I were the only sophomores, allowed to tag along only because our parents made our older siblings bring us. Even though I tried to act like it was no big deal, sitting in the front seat of my effortlessly cool older brother's car with two hot girls in the back seat felt pretty awesome.

That I looked up to Johnny was an understatement. He was so smart, the kindest guy you would ever meet, and one flash of his smile would melt
~~~

any girl's heart. Even though we looked almost nothing alike – he took after our dad with dark hair, bright blue eyes, and a slighter build, while I got my mom's curly blond hair, dark eyes, and more muscular build – from the very start I wanted to be just like Johnny.

I proudly marveled at Johnny that day; he was completely in his element, clearly the leader of the group, telling everyone when and where to meet up, mapping out the runs and lifts we would take. We all followed him like ducklings. Even Jules, who I knew preferred to be the one calling the shots, fell in line, falling under Johnny's charismatic spell just like everyone else.

Late in the afternoon, I was halfway down a run when I spotted Johnny, his green and white striped beanie easily recognizable. He was splayed out on the snow, his skis and poles scattered across the slope. Garage sale, I *chuckled to myself. I snickered as I made my way over to him, ready to rib him a bit for wiping out. But as I approached him I noticed his eyes were closed. And as I looked closer my heart filled with dread when I saw the trickle of blood coming from his nose.*

"Johnny?" I croaked. He didn't move. "Johnny!" I shouted. I felt paralyzed, too terrified to move. The next thing I knew Jules was kneeling next to Johnny. She placed her ear near his mouth. "He's breathing," she said. Suddenly she was shouting at skiers passing by on the slope, "Hey you in the red hat! Yes, you! Go tell the ski patrol we need emergency medical on this run, now! And tell them we need an ambulance! Go! Now!"

Within a few minutes the emergency team had Johnny's limp body strapped to a ski patrol board and were maneuvering him down the mountain. They placed Johnny in the ambulance, and Callie, Jules, and I rushed to the car.

"Jake, give me your keys," Jules said forcefully. With trembling fingers I handed her the keys without question. We threw everything in the car as quickly as possible, then took off following the ambulance. It wasn't until the next day that I remembered Jules didn't even have a driver's license yet.

"Callie, call the Thompsons. Tell them what happened and that we're heading to St Charles," Jules ordered. I hadn't even noticed when she had

asked the paramedics what hospital they were going to.

Callie made the call, her voice choppy with emotion. "They'll meet us there," she informed us with difficulty, tears streaming down her face. Jules reached toward the back seat, and Callie took her hand for a moment, then released her, scolding, "Two hands on the wheel, Jules."

We arrived at the hospital just a few minutes after my parents did. They were quickly taken back to see Johnny and to find out from the doctor what the CT scan had found. Callie, Jules, and I could only wait helplessly. When my parents came back their faces were drawn in a way I had never seen.

"It's... it's not looking good," my mom choked out. "They're taking him to surgery to try to relieve the pressure under his skull... but..." she trailed off.

"All we can do now is hope," my dad said, pulling my mom into his arms and beckoning me toward him, pulling me into the embrace. "Jules, Callie, you girls head home. Your dad is probably worried about you," he said gently over the top of my head.

Before she left, Jules came over to me and hugged me tightly. "Thank you, Jules," I mumbled through the tears that I couldn't hold back anymore. She had been incredible, knowing exactly what to do in a crisis; if it hadn't been for her I would still be standing frozen on that mountainside. I watched her and Callie walk out of the hospital holding each other. I'll never forget watching Jules, the younger sister, rub Callie's back and smooth her hair in such a motherly way.

A few hours later a doctor delivered the news that would change my life forever. My brother, my hero, my best friend, was gone.

~~~

I run my thumb along the palm of Jules's hand, trying to offer what little comfort I can. "I'm fine, Jules. Just a bit beat up."

She roughly scrubs at her tears. "Then stop being an ass and call your mom," Jules growls at me, dropping my hand and stomping out of my bedroom.
~~~

CHAPTER 18

Jake

I spend the next ten minutes wallowing in self-pity. *Why did she have to come here? Why did she have to see me like this?* I keep expecting to hear Jules leave, hoping that she will but dreading that she does. I run my one mobile hand across my face. *You can do this. Just say it.* I take one painful breath then call out, "Jules?"

She appears in my doorway, arms crossed. "What?" she asks with a scowl.

"I think I need your help." I see the small smirk on her face. After all the crap I have given her for needing to be OK with asking for help, she must really be enjoying this. "Can you help me get up? I want to sit in the living room." She just stares at me. "Please," I say.

I realize self-consciously that I'm shirtless, something that I've never been embarrassed about before. *At least I'm wearing sweatpants, or else this would be a whole new level of mortifying,* I think to myself.

She walks over silently and together we manage to get me to a sitting position and my arm into a sling with only a little groaning on my part. I'm very aware of Jules's hands on my bare skin, but she seems completely unfazed.

Once I'm up I'm fine walking into the living room. I eye the couch. Jules stares at me silently. She's not going to make this easy on me. "Can you help me again? Please?" She waits silently. "I want to sit on the couch." Jules grabs a few pillows and sets them up against the arm of the couch as a sort of backrest then helps ease me onto the couch so that I'm sitting up with my legs stretched out.

"Now was that so hard?" she asks with false sweetness.

"Sitting up and sitting down? Yes, it was incredibly hard. You try doing that with a broken collarbone," I say wincing as I adjust myself on the couch.

"No," Jules snaps, her voice hard. "Talking to me. Telling me what you want. Was *that* so hard?" she says her eyes narrowed at me. I'm preparing for her to lecture me, but she turns and walks away.

I rub my eyes in frustration with my mobile hand. *Yes. Telling you what I want is so hard I don't think I can do it.*

A few minutes later Jules walks back into the living room carrying a plate with a sandwich on it. "Eat half then you take these," she says, placing a few pills on my plate. She sits on the coffee table in front of me. After I've eaten my half sandwich and gulped down the pills, Jules writes something down on a notepad, which I assume must be the medication log she mentioned.

After I've finished the second half of my sandwich she takes the plate from me. I grab her hand with my good arm.

"Jules." She keeps her eyes trained on the plate. "Jules, look at me." She slowly meets my gaze. "I'm sorry, OK. I'm sorry."

She places the plate on the coffee table and perches gently on the couch next to me. "Sorry for what?" she asks. *She is* really *not going to make this easy on me.*

"For scaring you," I say, starting with the easiest apology. "It's not like I went out and *tried* to break my collarbone," I add with a forced laugh.

She nods. "Anything else?" she asks, needling me for more.

"For…" I close my eyes, unable to look at her, "for kissing you on the mountain. I shouldn't have done that. I'm sorry." I finally open my eyes and I'm surprised by the expression on her face. She looks even more exasperated with me than before.

"That's not why I'm mad at you, Jake!" she shrieks at me.

"It's not?" I ask confused.

"Don't you ever listen to anything I say?"

"You say a lot of things. There's only so much I can retain," I say, making a lame joke. She glares at me. *Not the time for jokes, Jake.*

"All I wanted you to do was talk to me. I told you that you caught me off guard. And that I was sorry for how I reacted. And if you had just talked to me like I asked you then maybe I would have told you that I wanted you to try it again. When I was more prepared!"

Wait, what? "You would have?" I ask, sounding like an idiot even to my own ears.

"If you had just talked to me then yes, I would have! It's been over a decade since I shared a first kiss with someone and I just..." her voice loses some of its fire, "ruined it." Anger returns to her voice as she continues, "But you skied off and then refused to talk to me and even yelled at me. And now... now I don't know what to think," she says, her voice softening and her eyes turning away from me.

I haven't released her hand through any of her lecture. I squeeze her hand and her gaze returns to my face.

"I'm sorry for not talking to you. I was... Well, I was a coward. I thought I had finally and completely ruined things between us and I was so ashamed I just wanted to run away from it," I admit. *Maybe I should embrace the way the dose of heavy painkillers seems to be loosening my tongue.*

She stares at me warily. "I have to understand what's going on. I need to know how you feel. About me."

I gulp reflexively. *Can I finally tell her?* "How I feel about you?" I reach up and hesitantly tuck a loose curl behind her ear. "You...are everything."

~~~

A few days after Johnny died, I was sitting on the swing in my back
~~~

yard. *"Need a push?"* I heard a familiar voice call from across the yard. I looked up to see Jules crossing the yard, offering a tentative half-smile.

"Hey," I said trying to make my voice sound light, but very much failing.

"Your mom said you were back here."

"What are you doing here?"

"I was just dropping off dinner. My dad made a pot roast. Callie wasn't up to it, so he asked me to deliver it."

"That was nice of him. Thanks," I said, but my voice sounded hollow.

"Don't say that until you've tried it," Jules said with a grin.

I stared at the ground, unsure of what to do, what to say, unsure of everything.

"Do you want to go somewhere?" Jules asked.

I looked up at her surprised. *"Like where?"*

"Anywhere. Your yard is always beautiful, but I think you might need a change of scenery."

"No thanks," I mumbled.

"Do you mind if I stay a while?" she asked undeterred.

"I'm not much company right now, Jules. And I definitely don't feel like talking about... anything," I muttered.

"I talk enough for the both of us," she said with a small smile.

I looked up at her. *"There's no denying that,"* I replied, finding something even mildly funny for the first time in days.

"So, do you need a push?" she asked again.

I shrugged. *"Why not."*

Jules stood behind me and grabbed the ropes of the swing. She whispered in my ear, *"I'm here for you, Jake. Through anything, I'm here for you."* I nodded silently.

Jules trying to push me in the swing did not go so well. She didn't pull back on the swing so she could barely move me, then I ended up swinging sideways, then I almost tipped out of the swing. I was laughing so hard my sides hurt and Jules had tears of laughter streaming down her face. We gave up on the swing.

When she tried tossing me a football, her toss was so pathetically awful I ended up doubling over and dropping to my knees I was laughing so hard. *"This is why I don't play throwing sports!"* she called attempting *another pathetic toss that had the football turning end over end and was horribly off target.*

My mom came outside to investigate what had us howling in laughter; Jules demonstrated with another toss of the football that actually set my mom giggling, too.

"Do you want to stay for dinner, Jules dear?" my mom asked. I looked at Jules expectantly. She had actually brought some glimmer of life into our home and I wasn't ready for her to leave and take that glimmer with her.

"That's really kind of you, Mrs. Thompson, but if you're having my dad's pot roast..." I felt my shoulders slump in disappointment.

"We can have that tomorrow. Tonight we can have a lasagna the Johnsons dropped off," my mom suggested.

"Oh, in that case, thank you I would love to stay for dinner," Jules said brightly.

"What's wrong with your dad's pot roast?" I asked as we walked inside.

"Nothing. I've just had it at least 50 times in the past year. And the year before that. And I am more than a little tired of it. But for you I might actually have suffered through another pot roast."

"Oh how magnanimous of you," I said teasingly, but my heart soared as I kept replaying her words over and over in my head. 'For you.'

~~~

"Now I have to ask you," I say, my heart pounding. "How do you feel about me?"

Jules looks away from me, and I feel my heart sink.
~~~

CHAPTER 19

Jake

Her eyes trained on the floor, Jules says softly, "It's hard to admit, even to myself, that I have feelings for you, Jake." *I know the feeling. Wait. Does that mean she has feelings for me?* "Because for so long I couldn't let myself feel that way about you," she admits. *Again, I know the feeling.*

"There was a time, a long time ago, when I thought maybe we had something. I thought that *you* knew how I felt about you then," she says giving me a sidelong look that makes me squirm.

I want to deny it but I can't. I had a pretty strong inkling about how she felt about me then. The same way I felt about her.

"But you made it so clear that we were only friends. Completely platonic. That I was nothing more than a friend to you. It hurt, really hurt, seeing you with so many girls, so many of my friends."

My heart aches knowing that I hurt her in any way. That the choices I made trying to stop myself from hurting her still caused her pain.

"I had to build up so many walls around my heart because of you. And honestly without Dylan, the way he made me feel about myself, I don't know if those walls would ever have come down."

Seeing her with Dylan, how happy she was, I knew that he was the right guy for her. That staying away from her then was the best thing I could have done for her. Even if it tore me apart.

"I had to build my own walls against you, Jules. And it's taken me a long time to bring those walls down," I admit.

~~~

"Please take care of her. Of them. My girls. Please take care of them," Dylan said, eyes still trained on the door.

My voice cracked as I answered. "You know I will. I would do anything for your girls, Dylan."

His lips curled up in a small smile. "I know you would, Jake."

He sat silently for a long stretch of time, seemingly lost in his thoughts. I had no idea what to say. What do you say to your dying best friend? The silence stretched on, the hums and beeps of the various machines and monitors the only sounds in the room.

"I have something I need to tell you," Dylan said finally. "Something I thought I would never tell you. But now there's no point in not telling you," he said, eyes never leaving the door.

"OK," I said slowly, a bit concerned. "Shoot."

"I've always known."

"Known what?" I asked, confused.

"How you feel about her." My breath caught.

After a too-long pause, I started to reply, "Dylan, I don't know what you're talking about-"

"It's no use denying it now," he cut me off, his voice barely above a whisper. He finally turned and looked me in the eye, without the anger I expected, perhaps even with pity. "I always knew. That first day I met her, I knew how you felt about her. I shouldn't have pursued anything with her, because I knew, even if you wouldn't admit it, that you were crazy about her." I had my eyes trained on my hands, unable to face the truth even then. "But I liked her too much I couldn't help myself," he said with a small chuckle. "And then, I guess you understand better than anyone," he continued, "I couldn't stop myself from falling in love with her."

"Dylan, Jules and I never, she has never…" I trailed off, unable to put
~~~

my turbulent thoughts into coherent words.

"I know that. I do. I just wanted you to know that I always knew. And that I never thought less of you for it. Because, honestly, how could anyone not be in love with her."

"I don't know what I'm supposed to say," I replied helplessly, because what do you say when your best friend finally tells you he knows you've been in love with his wife for at least a decade.

"Just say that you'll take care of her."

I swallowed, catching my breath before I could say the words. "I will. I always will. Because I love you." He was my best friend. My hero. And far too soon I would have to learn to face life again having lost two brothers.

~~~

Jules finally looks at me, tilting her head to one side like she's studying me. "I keep wondering if this is some weird guilt-driven attempt to keep your promise to Dylan to take care of me. Is that what this is, Jake? Do you just feel obligated to take care of me and this is how you think you should take care of me?"

I let out a long sigh. "No, Jules, if anything guilt is what has been keeping me away from you for so long." *What should maybe keep me away from you now.*

"What does that mean, Jake?" she asks, her eyes searching mine. "I don't understand. And now Callie says that you've always had feelings for me. That this isn't something new that you're feeling for me. And I just don't understand how that can possibly be true. When you had your chance with me so long ago and you never ..." she trails off holding her hands up helplessly.

How do I explain this? How do I make her understand that I've always cared about her? That staying away from her was what I needed to do, for her sake, even if it nearly broke me.

"Jules, I never took that chance because I never wanted to hurt you. I knew you deserved so much more than I could give. After Johnny..." I have to take a deep breath before I can continue. It's so hard to talk about him, to remember losing him. I haven't even said
~~~

his name aloud in so long. "After Johnny I was hurting so much and I was trying to escape that pain in the worst ways." I shudder thinking about what my parents went through during that time – the devastation of losing one son and watching their other son nearly self-destruct in the wake of it.

"I was such a hurricane of destructive choices then, and you were the eye of my hurricane. My center. I could destroy everything around you, but never touch you."

She tilts her head to the other side. "So you hurt me … to protect me … from you hurting me?"

"Well when you put it that way…" I say sarcastically, and we both laugh, the tension in the room lessening considerably.

"Then why have things changed now?" she asks.

What *has* changed? Why do I feel like I might actually have a shot to do things right with Jules now?

"Because *I've* changed. Because I'm not the teenage wrecking ball I once was. Because I like the person I am now. Because I finally have some hope that I might be something close to worthy of you. And now my only goal is to try to measure up, to keep trying to deserve you."

"Oh," she whispers, and I see some of the tension drain from her, like maybe she's heard me, accepted what I had to say, that she believes me.

"But you still haven't answered my question," I say with a lopsided smile. "How do you feel about me?"

Her eyes linger on her hand that is still entwined with mine, her brow slightly furrowed.

"These past few months I have felt something shift between us. And I guess I've tried to ignore it, because I didn't think there was any way you could possibly feel something more than friendship for me. But the truth is I do feel something more for you." Her eyes, sparkling with unshed tears, meet mine.

"You make me so happy, Jake. And I never thought I would feel that way ever again." She pauses and I feel like my only chance at happiness depends on her next few words. "And I want to give this a shot."

I let out the breath I've been holding. "Really?" I ask with a huge, dopey, can't-help-myself grin on my face.

"Really," she says shyly.

"I should have talked to you before I kissed you," I admit sheepishly. Jules gives me a look that seems to say *You think?* I shrug, or the equivalent of a shrug with only one mobile shoulder. "And it probably won't happen anytime soon, because…" I gesture at my sling as explanation, "But I hope you will give me a chance to try again sometime."

"I can wait," she says, a hint of pink reaching her cheeks.

She runs her fingers gently over my stubbled cheek. Then I notice her staring at my bare chest.

"Like what you see, Nelson?" I ask with a smirk, trying lamely to cover some of my discomfort over being so emotionally and physically bare in front of her.

"Actually I was thinking you look a lot harrier than the last time I saw you shirtless."

I gape at her. "What?" Is she really commenting on my body hair at a moment like this?

"You even have back hair now," she says stretching her neck to look around my shoulder. "I don't remember you having that before," she adds, eyes twinkling with mischief.

"OK, enough out of you," I say, rolling my eyes.

"No really, Jake, what happened? Did you forget to shed your winter coat for the spring? Or are you just slowly transforming into an orangutan?" she asks, her voice full of laughter.

"If I could throw this pillow at you, Nelson, I would," I growl at her.

She gives me a mischievous smile then leans over and plants a kiss on my cheek. Then she whispers into my ear, "And I do like what I see."

CHAPTER 20

Jake

Over the next few days, Jules is in and out of my house frequently. She comes to check on me on her lunch break, stops by after work, looking over my medication log, leaving once she is sure I'm fed and comfortable. One night, when I'm feeling a little better, she brings Evie with her and the three of us have dinner in the living room – me on the couch, Evie and Jules sitting around the coffee table. Evie keeps asking me to retell the story of how I broke my collarbone. Each retelling becomes more harrowing. I even draw her a cartoon of my misadventure; the dialogue in the word bubbles mostly consists of "Ow!" and "Argh!"

After dinner, Jules wanders over to the corner of the room. I'm busy telling the most exciting part of the story, when the ski patrol whisked me down the hill strapped to the medical board, when I hear the soft tones of guitar chords. I awkwardly maneuver myself to look over to the corner and see Jules strumming my guitar, singing softly to herself. She stops suddenly.

"Why'd you stop," I ask, trying not to sound too disappointed.

She looks up, smiling shyly. "Out of tune," she explains, as she begins to tune the instrument string by string. When she is satisfied she begins to play again, singing softly to herself.

"We want to hear," I call beckoning her to come closer. She stands, still strumming and sits on the coffee table.

"Any requests?" she asks, her question directed at both Evie and me.

"A fast song!" Evie squeals. Jules complies with a rockin' rendition of The Wheels on the Bus.

After she finishes the song, Evie and I cheer and applaud. Or I applaud by slapping my thigh with my mobile hand. I reach over and grab Jules's knee. "I haven't heard you play in so long, Jules."

She shrugs. "I haven't felt much like playing until recently," she admits, her eyes meeting mine.

"Why recently?"

She smiles shyly. "You." *Oh.* I take her hand and bring it to my lips for a quick kiss on her palm. Jules grins more broadly at me. "Any more requests?" she asks, strumming a chord.

Two weeks after my injury I'm back at work. I learn quickly how difficult most tasks are when done one-handed; I'm also grateful that I'm right-handed and my injury is limited to my left side. My day is going fine, but I have something in mind that is making me antsy and time just seems to drag. I glance at the clock every few minutes, willing the time to pass.

By 3:30 I can't wait any longer. I call Jules. Even though I know she's still at work, I can't wait any longer.

"Hi," she answers, a softness to her voice that does things to me.

"Hey," I say nervously. "I was wondering… If you don't have plans… Would you want to grab dinner Friday night?"

"Jake Thompson are you asking me out?" she teases me.

I grin into the phone. "Yeah, Jules, I am."

I step out of the car and walk to the passenger side to open the door for Jules. As she steps out of the car smiling at me, she reaches for my one mobile hand, and we walk to her door, fingers entwined.

Jules fishes her keys out of her purse and unlocks the door.

Before opening the door, she turns back to me. "Thank you for tonight, Jake," she says, her eyes locked with mine. I stare at her, completely unsure of what to do. The way she's smiling at me, the moonlight in her blond hair, the way she's been flirting with me all night - all I want to do is kiss her. But the last time I tried that, things didn't go so well.

She tugs at my hand, offering me a sly smile. I let out a breath of relief and lean in to kiss her, and this time she kisses me back.

Jules pulls back slightly and murmurs in a low voice, "Do you want to come in?"

I groan inwardly, and a bit outwardly, too. "I want to," I say honestly. "But I can't."

She looks up at me through her long lashes, silently trying to make me change my mind.

"I can't," I repeat, with a small laugh, though I feel a little less convinced. "I'm still injured," I say gesturing lamely at my sling.

Having a broken collarbone has actually been helpful, because it has forced us to wait on anything physical. Jules and I have the chance to focus on building the emotional side of our relationship, and I have come to realize that's something really important to me. Having a relationship at all is something new to me, and I want to do things right.

"And even though I've made some progress with your dad, I think he is still ready to chase me off with his shotgun," I add, not entirely joking.

Jules tugs me closer, kissing me more deeply. "Are you sure?" she whispers.

"Don't make this harder than it already is," I groan in frustration.

She presses her body against me and says with a wicked grin, "That's the idea," making me groan in a completely different way. I kiss her again and pull her tighter against me, losing myself in the moment. I mistakenly pull her against my bad arm too tightly, making me yelp in actual pain. Jules jumps back suddenly, her eyes flashing with alarm.

"I...I'm sorry. Just got a little carried away," she says with a shaky laugh.

"I did, too," I say, wincing and adjusting my arm in its sling. "But mostly I blame you," I add with a wink.

"That's fair," she concedes with a sly grin. "Do you need to come inside for an ice pack?" she asks innocently.

"No, I don't," I grumble. "And I know what you're doing. I'm going home," I say narrowing my eyes at her. Jules feigns innocence, but the small smirk on her face is a giveaway. I let out a breath in frustration. "This cockblock will be gone in a few weeks," I say gesturing to my sling.

"Cockblock? Aren't you presumptuous, Mr. Thompson," she says with mock astonishment.

"It's an expression," I say rolling my eyes. *Sort of.* I bend low to whisper in her ear. "We can pick up where we left off once this *cockblock* is gone."

"Stop saying that," she giggles.

I wait a beat. "Cockblock," I deadpan, making her laugh out loud.

She gives me one last chaste kiss on the cheek before she walks into the house. I hear her lock the door behind her. I let out the breath I've been holding. I walk down the path, chuckling to myself that it's a good thing she walked away when she did because my resolve was definitely waning.

Jules

I look at the clock in my bedroom and see that it's only 9:30. I chuckle to myself seeing the time because it felt like Jake and I were out so late. *We're so old.*

I change quickly into my usual pajama shorts and t-shirt and slip into bed, pulling out a book to read. I feel a bit chilly and think I'll grab my robe or a sweatshirt to warm up. A rascally idea pops into my head. I grab my phone.

JULES: I can't sleep. It's too cold. Can you warm me up?

I wait a few minutes, but I don't see a response from Jake. I figure he's either still driving home or more likely choosing not to respond. I sigh, resigned, and pull back the covers to grab a sweatshirt. It was a long shot.

Then I hear the tap at my bedroom's sliding glass door.

My heart racing, I open the door as quietly as possible. Jake steps in and starts taking off his shoes and jacket. "I am only here to serve as source of body heat. Human heater that is it. Is that clear?" he asks, his expression somewhere between amused and annoyed. I nod innocently; Jake can't see that my fingers are crossed behind my back.

CHAPTER 21

Jules

I hear a timer go off in the kitchen. *I didn't set a timer. What's that for?* I ask myself.

"Jules can you get that?" Callie calls from the sink. "My hands are dirty."

"Sure, just a second," I say walking into the kitchen and turning off the timer on Callie's phone. "What's that timer for?" I ask.

"The oven," she says, still busy washing at the sink. "Can you grab it?"

I put on oven mitts and open the oven door. I stand up, confused by what I see. "What is that?" I ask, making a face.

"Well what does it look like?" Callie asks, looking at me like I'm incredibly dense.

"Um… a hamburger bun?"

"That's right. And where is it?" she asks, her voice a bit patronizing.

"In the oven…" *A bun in the oven?* "Oh my God!" I shriek whirling on Callie who is beaming at me. "Are you…Are you pregnant?!" I scream. She nods silently, her huge smile only growing wider. In an instant I am holding my sister. My beautiful, funny, kind, strong, brilliant, amazing sister. When I first grab her we are both giggling uncontrollably, but soon we are a sobbing puddle still clinging to each other as we rock on the floor.

Evie walks into the kitchen to investigate the commotion. "What's wrong? Why are you crying?" she asks, her eyes wide with alarm.

I reach my arm out to her and pull her into our weeping pile on the floor. "We're just so happy, baby. We're just so happy," I say, kissing the top of her head at least a dozen times.

"If you're so happy why are you crying?" Evie asks, still eyeing Callie and me warily.

"Because sometimes you can feel so happy that the happiness explodes out of your eyes. Like a volcano," Callie says matter-of-factly. Then she pantomimes joy exploding out of her eyes complete with explosion sound effects. Evie and I both crack up. Callie is going to be the best mom.

Callie is going to be a mom, I repeat to myself, smiling like a fool. For nearly two years Callie and Ryan have been trying to get pregnant. I know there have been so many times she has felt like giving up. Though she's never said it, I'm sure there have been plenty of moments she's resented me for getting pregnant without even trying to. And now it's finally happening.

I mouth silently to Callie, '*Can I tell her?*' Callie nods, eyes twinkling.

"Evie, sweet pea, you are going to be a big cousin."

She tilts her head, trying to understand.

"Your Auntie Callie is going to have a baby!"

"A baby?" Evie squeals. "Can it be a girl? I want to play ponies with the baby."

Callie laughs. "We won't know if the baby is a boy or girl for a few months. But boy or girl, they will always want to play ponies with you." Evie seems satisfied with this answer and skips out of the kitchen.

Callie and I take a few more minutes to blubber together. I ask her a million questions about her due date, when she found out, how she told Ryan, how she is feeling. We eventually dry our tears and join the rest of the family in the living room; our red-rimmed eyes and tear-stained faces must be quite a sight.

My dad, Ryan, and Jake barely glance at Callie and me as we enter the room; they are too enthralled by Evie turning cartwheels and somersaults as she prattles on about her favorite pony cartoon.

For the past few weeks Jake has been joining us for Tuesday night dinners. At first I worried what my family might think about Jake and me being together. But it was like they had already made up their minds about us - before *I* had made up my mind about us – and Jake joining us for family dinners was just assumed. Evie and I have been joining the Thompsons for dinner on Thursday nights, and they have been beyond welcoming. I've spotted Jake give Debbie a few looks that seem to be warning her to tone down her enthusiasm, which has just made me love him and her even more.

I settle onto the couch next to Jake and tuck myself into his right side. Jake's sling is off and he's recovered considerably, which has been…um…fun. But he is still favoring his left side a bit, so I tend to drift toward his right side so that he's more comfortable.

"Callie's pregnant," I whisper to him, grinning.

"I heard," he says pulling me close. "I think the whole neighborhood heard, blabber mouth," he says teasing me. I did have quite the excited outburst. "That's wonderful," he says, dropping a kiss to the top of my head. "Auntie Jules," he says, punctuating my new title with another kiss.

"And Uncle Jake," my dad says from his seat across the room.

Jake and I both turn our heads to my dad, startled by his words. He just smiles benignly at us. I glance up at Jake, he swallows reflexively, like he's holding back some strong emotion. With those three words, it's like my dad offered Jake what he has been hoping for: acceptance.

There's no doubt in my mind that's where this is headed. That Jake will be part of this family, that he is already my family. But for now I am going to be happy in the present; I am going to just enjoy falling in love with my best friend.

I place a chaste kiss on Jake's cheek. But when our eyes meet he winks at me with a smile that promises more, and I try my best not to blush.

Jake

I have been looking forward to Friday night all week and now that it's here I'm starting to feel nervous. Tonight is Evie's first sleepover at my house. *And Jules is coming, too,* I remember almost as an afterthought, chuckling to myself.

I have all the ingredients for Evie's favorite homemade pizza. I have lots of animated kids' movies queued up on the streaming service; I'll have to remember to thank my mom and dad for sharing their login info with me. Most importantly, I spent a great deal of time Wednesday night assembling the twin bed that now stands in my previously empty spare room. I hope Evie likes the unicorn bedding.

"Alright Evelyn, I believe it is your bedtime," Jules informs Evie and me at least an hour after Evie's normal bedtime.

"Aw already?" Evie asks in protest. I have to bite my tongue not to do the same.

We have been having so much fun I completely lost track of time. Or I didn't *want* to know what time it was so I didn't check. *Way to be the adult, Jake.* I'm almost surprised Jules didn't say, 'Evelyn *and Jacob,* I believe it is your bedtime.'

"I'll put Evie to bed," I say to Jules.

"Yes! Jake can read me a story!" Evie squeals, bouncing up and down.

Jules opens her mouth to say something, but I hold my hand up to stop her. "I've got this," I say confidently. I lower my voice so that only she can hear. "Pour yourself a glass of wine and go enjoy a moment to yourself on the porch. I'll join you shortly," I add dropping a kiss to her cheek. She smiles an enigmatic smile and kisses Evie goodnight.

After far too many books and several retellings of my legendary ski accident, I finally am able to kiss Evie goodnight and close her bedroom door. I realize now that Jules was smiling because she knew I wouldn't be joining her 'shortly.'

Through the glass door that leads to the back porch, I see Jules leaning against the railing watching the setting sun. Standing on my back porch, wrapped in one of my jackets, in the light of the evening sun, she's never looked so beautiful. I open the door, and she turns to me with a small smile that confirms my suspicions that she knew saying goodnight to Evie would take much longer than I expected. She holds out her hand beckoning me to come closer, and I can't help my mischievous thoughts as I rush to her. I haven't seen Jules in a few days, and all evening I've been looking forward to some alone time.

Jules, however, does not seem to share my baser thoughts at the moment, and begins to tell me all about her day at work. I do my best to distract her as she tells stories from her work day, but she barely seems to register my affections. Standing in front of her, I brush her hair back from her face, drop soft kisses to her forehead and cheeks; all the while she is talking. I grip her waist tightly, and she keeps talking. When I place a kiss on her mouth, she stops talking only momentarily then continues with her story. I can't help but laugh.

"What?" Jules asks, stopping her story mid-sentence.

"If you haven't noticed, I'm trying to make out with you," I say more entertained than anything.

"Is that what you're doing? Well let me finish my story first," she says, completely unaffected by my charm. *What an ego boost*, I think laughing aloud.

Still laughing, I lean my forehead on hers. "That's why I love you. You always-"

"Wait wait wait," Jules interrupts me, angling away from me with a grin. She places both of her hands on the sides of my face so that I have to look directly at her. "Reverse. Say that again," she orders.

"What?" I ask with a frown, covering one of her hands with mine, unsure of what I said that caught her attention.

"Say that again," she repeats, looking up at me through her long lashes, sliding her hands behind my neck, tracing small circles on the exposed skin.

Oh, that. I gulp reflexively. "You mean, 'That's why I love you?'" I ask hesitantly.

She smiles coyly at me. "Just the last part," she says, her voice softening.

"But I've told you that before," I reply, almost defensively. *Haven't I? Or have I just thought it so many times I feel like she should know?*

"No, you haven't," she says with a small shake of her head, the movement of her hands halting abruptly. "You've told me you have feelings for me, that you're crazy about me, that I'm *everything*, but never…that." *Oh.*

"Well, I do," I say, tightening my hold on her waist, hoping the shaking of my voice doesn't betray how terrified I am.

"Then tell me," Jules insists, her voice low, her dark eyes locked with mine.

I take a steeling breath. "I love you, Jules." I hold my breath, waiting for her reaction.

For what feels like an eternity, Jules says nothing, her gaze intense but giving nothing away. "Good," she finally says, with a small smile. My heart nearly stops. *Is that all she's going to say? I say 'I love you' and she says 'Good?'*

"Because I love you, too," she adds, with a mischievous grin. I close my eyes in relief, shaking my head at her entirely intentional torture of my poor, insecure heart. *She loves me. She really does love me.* I feel Jules brush her lips against mine, a small giggle escaping from her throat. I pull her flush against me, losing myself in this perfect moment with this incredible, maddening woman who I love completely.

CHAPTER 22

Jake

Evie and I are waiting at the bottom of the run for Jules. "Why is she always so slow?" Evie grumbles. I laugh. Even though it's only her second season skiing, Evie loves to bomb it down the ski slopes, just like me.

"Your mom just likes to enjoy every run to its fullest," I explain, though I also grumble to myself about her slow pace at times. "Here she comes," I say, recognizing Jules's bright green helmet.

"Good. Let's meet her at the lift," Evie says turning around.

"No. Let's wait for her here," I say hurriedly, grabbing Evie's arm lightly. Evie frowns at me.

"Why?" she asks, annoyed.

"Just because," I sigh. "You'll see."

Evie shrugs, somehow satisfied with my cryptic answer. "OK," she says and waits next to me.

Jules smiles at us as she approaches. "Hey you two snow bunnies," she calls.

My heart pounding, I use my pole to pop the latches on my ski bindings and step out of my skis.

"Done so soon? Don't you think we have time for one more

run?" Jules asks, surprised that I've taken off my skis.

I chuckle and smile like a fool, unable to hide my excitement. "Sure, we have time for another. But there's something I have to ask you first."

"OK?" Jules says slowly, clearly confused.

I unzip one of the many pockets on my jacket - the pocket I have checked at least four dozen times today – and pull out a small box. I kneel, which is something I couldn't do with my skis on. Jules's eyes narrow as she tries to figure out what I am doing. Then her eyes widen as she realizes why I'm kneeling in front of her with a small box in my hand.

"Jules Nelson, you are my best friend. The person who makes me want to be a better man. I have known most of my life that I needed you, that you were meant for me. It took me a long time to become the person who you needed. We have stood side by side through the most difficult and most incredible times of our lives. I want to spend my life with you. For us," I point to Evie, Jules, and me, "to be a family." I take a steeling breath, before I say the most exciting and terrifying four words I will ever say aloud. "Will you marry me?"

For once, Jules is at a loss for words. She nods slowly, and I can barely hear her whisper, "Yes."

I let out a loud *whoop* standing to kiss Jules. Then I turn to Evie and bounce her up and down chanting, "She said yes! She said yes!" Evie is laughing and shrieking as I bounce her, the skis still attached to her boots flopping about wildly. I set Evie on her skis and wrap both my girls in a hug, kissing Jules's cheek which is damp with rare tears. I mumble into Jules's ear, "Through anything."

EPILOGUE

Jake

Jules steps out of our closet in a simple black dress that is tight in all the right places.

"Oh, Ms. Nelson, when you're dressed like that you can't expect me to keep my hands off of you," I say with a mischievous grin, grabbing her and pulling her flush against me.

"You are trouble," Jules says, swatting my hands away playfully.

"Does that mean I'm being sent to the principal's office?" I ask in a low growl, grabbing her again and kissing her neck.

"Oh, behave," she says before leaning in for a lingering kiss.

"I will not behave," I say after we pull apart. "It's not every day I get to celebrate my wife's birthday."

We emerge from our bedroom to find Robert and Evie curled up on the couch, already busy reading a chapter book. "Thank you again, Dad, for watching Evie tonight," Jules says as she leans over, a bit precariously, and gives him a hug.

He kisses her on the cheek. "You look beautiful, darling. And I'm glad to do it. I hope you two have a great time. Pretty soon you won't have too many chances to go out to dinner," he says beaming at his daughter.

"Good night, sweet pea. I love you," I say kissing the top of Evie's head.

"Night, Dad. Love you," she says offhandedly. Nearly two years since Jules and I have been married and it still gives me a thrill hearing Evie call me Dad. It was Robert who came up with the idea that Dylan would be 'Daddy' and I would be 'Dad.'

We settle into the car, and I playfully check that Jules's seatbelt is latched. She shakes her head at me with a small, amused smile. I pretend like I'm joking, but I truthfully wanted to double-check; I have been a bit over-protective recently.

I lean over and kiss Jules. "I love you," I say placing another kiss on her cheek. Then I lean down and kiss her beautifully round belly. "And I love you," I say to the tiny person I can't wait to meet.

ABOUT THE AUTHOR

KC Weber is an educator with a passion for helping young people discover their love of language and the written word. In her twelve years (and counting!) in the classroom, she has taught every elementary school grade level from kindergarten through fifth grade, and she knows first-hand that nothing can prepare any teacher for the first week of kindergarten. She attended the University of North Carolina for her undergraduate studies and went on to earn a Master's of Teaching at Oregon State University and a Doctorate of Education at George Fox University in Oregon. Her other works include *The Pieces We Leave Behind* and *Something More*. She lives in Oregon with her husband and two children.

www.ingramcontent.com/pod-product-compliance
Lightning Source LLC
Chambersburg PA
CBHW070521160726
48003CB00004B/1654